SARAH PURDUE

◆

LOVE UNEXPECTED

Complete and Unabridged

LINFORD
Leicester

First published in Great Britain in 2017

First Linford Edition
published 2017

A catalogue record for this book is available
from the British Library.

ISBN 978–1–4448–3475–8

Published by
F. A. Thorpe (Publishing)
Anstey, Leicestershire

Set by Words & Graphics Ltd.
Anstey, Leicestershire
Printed and bound in Great Britain by
T. J. International Ltd., Padstow, Cornwall

This book is printed on acid-free paper

1

Jenny arrived at the boarding gate with only minutes to spare. The last few people were at the desk getting their boarding passes checked. Shifting the weight of her carry-on suitcase from one achy arm to another, she presented her boarding pass to the well-dressed airline representative, whose name-badge read 'Sebastian'. Sebastian took the pass and glanced at the list on the computer in front of him.

'And will Mr Dalton be travelling with you today?' Sebastian, who filled the airline uniform out in all the right places, looked up at Jenny.

'No,' Jenny said firmly, aware that another traveller had joined the queue she now found herself in.

'It appears that the tickets were booked at the same time?'

'Yes,' Jenny said through gritted

teeth, 'but Mr Dalton can no longer make the trip.' She tried to keep her face blank, holding back all the emotions she felt inside.

'I see,' Sebastian said, clearly hoping that Jenny would share what he considered to be some sort of juicy gossip. 'Passport, please.'

Jenny suppressed a groan. She wasn't used to travelling, especially alone, and she had assumed that she wouldn't need her passport again until she reached her destination.

'One moment, please,' she murmured, bending down and opening her carry-on suitcase.

She was rewarded with an audible sigh from Sebastian, and impatient shuffling from the man who was in the queue behind her. She could only see his feet, but they were dressed in tan loafers that screamed *expensive*. Jenny pushed a hand into the case, felt around, and pulled out her passport. As she was handing it over to Sebastian, she realised that a pair of silky red knickers had hitched a ride. Mortified, she attempted to grab them back from Sebastian, who had merely raised an eyebrow; but in her haste they sailed through the air and landed somewhere behind her.

Oh, please, no! she said silently to herself. *This is not happening!*

Jenny wondered for a moment if she could ignore what had just occurred and walk into the tunnel that led to the aircraft, pretending the knickers were not hers. It wasn't as if she had any need for sexy underwear anymore.

'I believe you dropped these?' a voice said behind her. It was warm-sounding but not mocking, and there was a trace of an accent that she couldn't place. Taking a deep breath and forcing her face into a bland smile, she turned on the spot and reached out a hand.

The man in the queue behind her was handsome . . . no, more than that — he was gorgeous. He was much taller than her; if she had to guess, she would say well over six feet. There was a leanness to him that spoke of being a regular sportsman. His skin was the colour of a latte, and he had jet-black hair, cut close to his scalp, which allowed his deep brown eyes to shine.

'Thank you,' Jenny managed to say in a high-pitched squeak before turning back round, shoving the offending knickers into the pocket of her jeans and wishing that a sinkhole would open up beneath her, or some other natural disaster occur.

'You're welcome,' the voice said, and this time there was definitely a hint of humour in it.

Jenny groaned inwardly, and forced herself to look up just high enough to see that Sebastian's hand was holding out her passport. She snatched it back, and then, head down, practically ran onto the plane, wanting to put as much distance between herself and yet another personal disaster as possible.

★ ★ ★

Jenny took another look at the boarding pass in her hand, hoping that she had made a mistake. The pass clearly said Row 24, Seat D. She was one of the last in the queue to get on the plane, and so most of the seats were already occupied by passengers trying to find both ends of their seatbelts or checking the in-flight magazine.

There was no mistaking it. The two empty seats stared back at her, complete with a small sign that read 'CONGRATULATIONS NEW MR & MRS!' Jenny knew she was blushing, but didn't really care. By now, it must be obvious to the entire plane that she was travelling alone, that there was no 'MR' — at least, not on this flight.

The couple in seats 'A' and 'B' had been beaming up at her, but when they saw her reaction, and took in the fact that there was no-one accompanying her, their faces dropped into the kind of supportive expression that Jenny knew she was trying to run away from. She reached out and roughly tore down the sign, gave the poor couple what she hoped was an *I'm okay, it's a bit of a funny story!* smile, and then hurriedly sat down. She could feel the eyes of other passengers on her, and knew that she would be the topic of conversation for the next ten minutes at least as everyone tried to guess what her tragic story was.

'Dumped at the altar, I reckon,' said two girls with impossibly orange tans in the row behind. Jenny did her best to ignore them as she tried to wrestle her hand luggage under the seat in front, but all she succeeded in doing was replacing the faint blush of embarrassment on her cheeks with the deep pink of effort and barely contained frustration. *I will not cry, I will not cry*, she told herself in her head, over and over again.

'Ma'am, you'll have to place your bag in the overhead locker, I'm afraid.'

Jenny took a deep breath and then looked up into the eyes of an immaculately dressed, perfectly-made-up air hostess

— or 'cabin crew', as they now preferred to be known. She forced herself to smile.

'Yes, I know. Thank you,' she added, although she had no idea why she was thanking the woman. *Yes, you do,* a voice said in her head. *You are completely unable to be rude, even if the situation deserves it.* Jenny sighed. The cabin-crew woman, whose namebadge read 'Jemima', was exchanging exasperated glances with another welldressed crewmate. She took a step back, which Jenny took as indicating that she should stand up — clearly, on this airline, you stowed your own baggage.

Jenny hefted the bag over her head and attempted to squeeze it in alongside the other luggage. As she pushed, standing on tiptoe since she was only five feet four, she could feel a bead of sweat run down her back and into the waistband of her jeans. Jemima looked on without any offer of help. Jenny gave up, knowing that the door wouldn't shut with the way she had left her bag, but no longer caring.

Jenny sat down and felt around for the two ends of her seatbelt, ignoring the icy gaze of Jemima, who had been forced to remove several pieces of luggage and rearrange them before she could close the compartment door. It felt to Jenny as if she were in a goldfish bowl, all eyes upon her. She reached into her pocket for her MP3 player, thinking that with music and closed eyes she could imagine herself somewhere else, when a heavy hand fell on her shoulder.

'Ma'am, I'm afraid electronic devices are forbidden until the captain announces we are at cruising height.'

It was Jemima again, and Jenny felt sure she was now on the 'difficult passenger' list, which meant she was unlikely to get her first choice of in-flight meal — or anything else she requested, for that matter.

'Sorry,' Jenny mumbled, pulling the headphones from her ears, wrapping them around the player, and pushing it safely into the seat-back pocket in front of her. Jemima gave one more unimpressed look in her direction, and then joined her colleagues walking up each aisle, checking that all tray tables were raised and all seatbelts were on. Jenny risked a quick glance out of the window as the aeroplane started to move towards the runway, and made unfortunate eye contact with the male half of the older couple sitting in the window seat. He reminded her so much of the look that her dad had given her when she had broken the news, that she had to close her eyes to hold back the tears. Digging her nails — which had been manicured for the special day, and still had the pale pink nail varnish and tiny crystals in place that her best friend and bridesmaid had insisted upon — into the palms of her hands, she repeated her mantra and willed her eyes to obey her.

Three hours into the flight, with a cup of coffee (she had requested tea) and no sugar to make it bearable (she hadn't even been offered any), Jenny knew that her bad luck was coming with her, however much she had hoped she would be leaving it behind with the disaster that was her life in recent weeks.

'Ladies and gentlemen, we will shortly be commencing service of dinner, so can we please request that if you have requested any special dietary requirements that you make yourself known to the cabin crew as they pass through the aircraft.'

Jenny watched as several lights flashed above seats, and wondered whether a vegetarian meal counted as a special requirement these days. With a morose sigh, and the feeling that whatever she decided it was probably wrong, she reached for the call button and pressed it. *Stop it*, she told herself firmly, *stop feeling so sorry for yourself*. Her self-lecture was interrupted by the lovely Jemima.

'Can I help you, ma'am?'

Jenny felt suddenly flustered.

'Er, yes. At least, possibly.'

Jemima raised a highly plucked eyebrow, which Jenny took as a sign to get on with what she had to say.

'I requested a vegetarian meal.'

'Yes, ma'am?'

'Well, I wondered whether it was classed as a 'special dietary requirement'?'

'No, ma'am. Will that be all?'

'Yes,' Jenny said, sliding down in her seat a little. 'Thank you,' she added as an afterthought, but Jemima was gone, stalking down the aisle to the front of the plane, no doubt to complain to her colleagues about the woman in Row 24, Seat D.

After dinner had been served and eaten, and cleared away with near-military swiftness, Jenny settled back in her seat, plugged in her headphones, and willed sleep to come. It didn't, of course. She couldn't actually remember the last time she had slept well. She opened her eyes and watched her fellow

11

passengers slowly drift off: some watching the in-flight movie, some tucked in with blankets and eye-masks. As if on cue, the lights in the main cabin were dimmed. Jenny closed her eyes again, and tried to practice some of the relaxation techniques that she knew.

'Would any medically trained staff please make themselves known to a member of cabin crew?' The voice sounded as if it was trying to be calm and reassuring, but also highlight the apparent urgency of the situation. A few of her fellow travellers stirred, and there was the low hum of voices around her.

Jenny sat up and pressed the call button. She had come away to have a break, but there was no way she was going to ignore a cry for help.

'We are rather busy at present, ma'am. If you are requesting a drink, I will need to come back later, I'm afraid.' It was Jemima again, and Jenny had to supress her moan.

'Actually, I'm a nurse. I work in the

emergency department at St. Jude's in London.'

This stopped Jemima in her tracks. Everyone had heard of St. Jude's: it was a world-renowned trauma centre, and Jenny was proud to work there. She watched with some satisfaction as Jemima's expression changed from impatient and irritated to surprised relief.

'Perhaps you could come with me. We have a passenger who is unwell.'

Jemima stepped back, and indicated that Jenny should make her way towards the front of the plane and First Class.

'Of course. I'd be happy to help.' Jenny's mind went quickly to nurse mode as she considered what the emergency might be, and what help she might be able to offer with the limited supplies available on a flight.

Jenny continued through the galley, and up to the curtain which separated First Class from Economy. A male member of the cabin crew stood there and blocked her way.

'She's a nurse,' Jemima said quickly from behind her, and the man stepped aside.

'At the front of the aircraft. A young boy. He seems pretty sick,' the crew member said. 'We have a doctor with him, but I think he could use another pair of trained hands.'

Jenny stepped through the curtain and up the wide aisle that led between the sofa-like seats to the front of the plane. A man was kneeling down on the floor, and Jenny could just make out the top of the boy's head and his worried parents who were crouched the other side of him.

'I'm Jenny Hale, an emergency nurse from St. Jude's. How can I help?' she said to the back of the man's head, assuming he was the doctor.

As he turned around to look at her, she felt her stomach lurch. It was the man in the queue behind her — the man she had basically thrown her knickers at.

2

Jenny and the man locked eyes for a heartbeat, and she knew that he recognised her. She fought down the groan. There were more important things to be worrying about right now — a sick little boy and his distraught parents — than her embarrassing escapades.

'Can you see if you can get a BP?' he asked suddenly.

'Of course,' Jenny said, all thoughts of their earlier embarrassing meeting pushed from her mind. She stepped around the man, and the boy's parents moved slightly so she could position herself near to their son.

She picked up a stethoscope from a small bag she assumed was the doctor's, and carefully slipped the blood-pressure cuff onto the young boy's arm.

'I'm Jenny,' she said as she worked. 'What's your name?'

The boy just stared at her, his eyes wide. His face was shimmering with sweat and his blond hair was ruffled.

'His name is Thomas — Tommy,' the boy's mother said. She had the same colouring as her son, fair and pale. 'He's eight,' she added, although she hadn't been asked.

Jenny smiled reassuringly at the woman before turning her attention back to her young patient.

'Tommy, I'm a nurse, and I'm just going to check your blood pressure. This cuff around your arm is going to get tight for a few seconds, OK?'

Tommy nodded but said nothing. His father reached out and smoothed his hair.

'Good boy, Toms,' he said softly.

Jenny worked swiftly, pumping up the cuff with one hand and holding the stethoscope in place with the other. She listened for the tell-tale heartbeat to appear and then disappear, to give her

16

the blood pressure.

'Seventy-five over forty, Doctor,' Jenny said, carefully keeping the concern from her voice.

'Call me Luc,' the man said, and Jenny nodded in acknowledgement.

'Is that bad?' the boy's father asked anxiously. 'Seventy over whatever?'

'It's a little on the low side,' Jenny said, risking a glance at Luc, who gave the smallest nod that neither parent seemed to notice. Luc's look told her to keep the parents talking so that he could continue to examine the boy.

'It tells us that Tommy is a little unwell. Can you tell me what happened?'

'He was fine when we got on board. He slept for a couple of hours, and then woke with a fever. He seemed to get poorly so quickly,' Tommy's mother said.

'Does Tommy have any health problems normally?' Jenny asked.

His mother shook her head.

'Has he been unwell recently?' Jenny said

Another shake of the head.

'He's been fine. So excited about the holiday . . . ' The mother's voice cracked a little. Jenny reached out a hand for her arm, and the other woman jumped at her touch.

'Does this hurt, Tommy?' Luc asked, gently pressing on the boy's stomach.

Tommy shook his head.

'Do you have pain anywhere?' Luc asked.

Again, another shake. Jenny reached for the electronic thermometer which was lying beside the boy's head. She gently ran the sensor over his forehead until she heard the beep.

'Temperature is thirty-eight point nine,' Jenny said, and the boy's parents gasped and exchanged worried looks.

Luc glanced at his watch.

'Was thirty-eight two, ten minutes ago.'

'Infection?' Jenny asked. Luc nodded, but appeared lost in thought, so Jenny didn't interrupt. He held out his hand, and she handed over the stethoscope that she had hooked round her neck out of habit. She watched as Luc listened to the boy's chest, and then, without needing to be asked, she helped the boy to sit up and lean forward.

'Can you take a deep breath, Tommy?' Luc asked.

Tommy did as instructed.

'Lungs are clear,' Luc said.

'What does that mean?' the boy's father asked, sounding agitated.

'It means that there is no sign of a chest infection or fluid build-up. That's good news, Mr — ?'

The man shook his head. 'John, my name's John.'

'It looks like Tommy has some kind of infection, John, which is why he is unwell,' Luc said, looking up from his examination. 'Can you just give us a minute? We'll be right back.'

Luc stood up, and with a nod indicated that Jenny should follow him. They walked back up the aisle and into the galley area.

'What do you think?' Jenny asked,

although she suspected that she already knew the answer.

'Infection of some kind, possibly sepsis.'

Jenny winced. Sepsis was bad news even if you were in a hospital with access to fluids and antibiotics — on a plane, it really didn't bear thinking about.

'I don't suppose you keep any kind of intravenous fluid on board?' Luc asked the senior cabin crew member who had just arrived.

Glen shook his head. 'Just a first aid kit and oxygen.'

Luc took this in and nodded. 'Can you set him up with some low-flow oxygen?'

Glen looked blank.

'Jenny here will help you.' She nodded. Addressing her, Luc continued, 'Can you see if you can find any signs of any wounds that might be the cause? And ask the parents where they have been and who Tommy might have been in contact with?'

Jenny nodded again. She wanted to ask what Luc would be doing, but didn't get a chance.

'I'm going to see what the on-board pharmacy has to offer,' he said with a thin smile.

Jenny frowned, and then watched as Luc picked up the intercom phone. For a moment she thought that Glen was going to object, but then he shrugged, clearly thinking better of it.

'Ladies and gentlemen, can I have your attention?' Jenny managed a small smile; he sounded like the very epitome of a consummate member of cabin crew.

'My name is Doctor Buchannan, and I have a request for you. We have a little boy who is unwell and in need of medication. If you have any medicines with you, please can I ask that you get them out and show them to me as I make my way through the plane?' He hung up the telephone and disappeared into Economy.

Jenny headed back to her patient, and

a few moments later Glen arrived with an oxygen mask and adapter. He ran the tubing to a section of panelling, which he removed, and then connected the line.

'Tommy, I'm going to put this mask on you. It has some special air for you to breathe.'

Tommy shook his head fiercely.

'It won't hurt you, I promise.' Jenny placed the mask over her own face and smiled. Tommy seemed to relax a little, and allowed Jenny to gently pull the mask over his head.

'I'm just going to have a look at you to see if you have any cuts on your legs and arms,' Jenny said. She started at Tommy's head and worked her way down his body, checking carefully for any cuts or wounds. When she got to his knees, she carefully rolled back the trousers on first his right and then his left leg. On his right knee was a plaster.

'I'm just going to pull this off,' she said to Tommy, aware that his parents were watching her every move closely, like a bird of prey after a rabbit. Jenny was used to this, and so continued with her job. Carefully, she peeled the plaster off, and could smell the infection even before she had a chance to look closely. The scent was sickly sweet, but with a sharp tang, and Jenny was sure she had found the reason why the boy was so unwell.

'I don't understand,' John said, 'it was healing up. I changed the plaster myself this morning. How did this happen? It was just a little cut.'

'Infections can develop quickly, particularly in children. Sometimes it doesn't matter how careful we are.' She looked at John, willing him to take on board her words. The last thing Tommy needed was his dad blaming himself when it was not his fault.

'I'm going to get something to clean it up, and the doctor is asking the other passengers if they have any antibiotics.'

Jenny stood up, and the boy's mother rose with her. 'Is there anything I can do? Please?' she asked desperately.

'Mrs — ?'

'Sonia, please call me Sonia.'

'I think Tommy needs his mum and dad to talk to him, distract him a little. I know you are worried, but the best thing for him right now is for you and John to believe that everything is going to be all right.'

Jenny smiled, even though her own insides were knotting. One thing was for sure: Tommy's situation was serious, and likely to get worse, but it wouldn't help John or Sonia to know that right now. Jenny maintained her expression as she held Sonia's gaze, the mother clearly searching her face for signs that she was withholding something. Satisfied for the moment, Sonia returned to her son, and started to ask him what he wanted to do when they arrived at their hotel.

Jenny found Luc in the galley of the plane with a wide mix of boxes and blister packs lined up on the side.

'Any antibiotics?' she asked.

He turned to her. 'A couple of

broad-spectrum ones.'

'I think I found the problem. Tommy has an infected wound on his knee. The dad said it was clean and healing before they left for the airport. Now it's oozing pus and smells infected.'

Luc let out a held-in breath and leaned back against the counter. He glanced at his watch.

'So, the wound has gone from healing fine to infected with signs of sepsis in five hours.'

Jenny nodded. 'Not good. What do you think?'

'We won't know for sure till we can get him to a hospital for testing, but what I'm worried about is a staph infection. It can take hold quickly and produce these kinds of symptoms.'

Jenny felt the colour blanch from her face. She had seen that before a few times, and the outcome had not always been positive. She looked at the choices of antibiotics on the side.

'Do you think they will work?'

Luc ran a hand through his short

hair. 'Maybe; we just have to hope it isn't a resistant form.'

'How far to the nearest hospital?' Jenny asked, although she suspected that she knew the answer.

'Five hours, if we divert.'

Jenny rubbed a hand across her face as if she could wipe away the worry and the new emotion, fear.

'Do you — '

Jenny didn't get any further with her question. The curtains had been yanked back and Sonia was there, panic in her eyes.

'There's something wrong with Tommy. He's started to go red, like a rash but in big patches.'

Luc gestured for Jenny to grab the tablets he had collected, and they both hurried back to their patient.

John was using a wet cloth to sponge his son's head, and Sonia pulled back her son's shirt. Jenny knelt beside Tommy as Luc picked up one of the boy's hands. The rash was present there, as well as across the boy's torso.

It looked like sunburn.

'Toxic shock syndrome.' Jenny whispered softly to Luc. Then, more loudly: 'Tommy, do you have a sore throat?'

Tommy swallowed and winced. That was all Luc and Jenny needed to know.

'Toxic shock syndrome,' Luc said, and Jenny felt her heart lurch as she gazed into the anxious faces of Tommy's parents.

3

'So now we know what it is, what do we do?' John said, looking from Luc to Jenny, desperate for a sign that things were not as bad as he imagined.

'Tommy is very sick,' Luc said, and Jenny saw what colour was left in Sonia's cheeks disappear. 'But there are things we can do.'

Sonia picked up the cloth, turned it over, and began to sponge her son's forehead, whilst John seemed trapped in despair.

'We need to get Tommy's temperature down — we have some medicine for that, and some antibiotics.'

'But he needs more than those,' John said, his voice flat and his teeth gritted.

Luc looked him straight in the eye. Jenny recognised the look. She had seen it before; sharing difficult news was one of the worse thing about working in medicine, but it had to be done, and there was a way to do it. Luc, it seemed, was an expert.

'In an ideal world, Tommy would be in hospital, but we are — ' He glanced at his watch. ' — over four and a half hours away from one. We are diverting. So we are going to do all we can to keep Tommy stable until we can get him the proper treatment.'

The words *all we can* were circling around in Jenny's head. Now she knew that Luc was as concerned about Tommy as she was. Those were the words that you used when you weren't sure what the outcome would be, but you wanted to offer some reassurance.

'Sonia, perhaps you could go and get some fresh cold cloths. John, I'm going to need your help to get Tommy to take some of the medicine. We only have capsules; can Tommy swallow tablets?'

Luc gave Jenny a grateful look, and Jenny nodded in acknowledgement. She knew very clearly that her role was not only to look after Tommy, but also his parents, who needed her almost as much as Tommy did. They also needed to feel useful, as if they were doing something for their son, and Jenny knew that she must keep them busy. Sonia stood up and headed for the galley.

'He can't manage tablets,' she said softly when she realised that John hadn't answered Jenny's question.

'Not a problem, we'll empty the capsules. Can you ask the flight attendant for some jam? It usually helps mask some of the taste.'

Sonia nodded, and then squeezed Jenny's shoulder as she walked past.

'John?' Jenny said, and reached over to touch John's shoulder. He jerked as if he had suddenly remembered where he was.

'Sorry,' he said, shaking his head as if he was mentally telling himself off.

'It's fine, John, you're doing fine. Perhaps you could help Tommy to sit up a little. It will be easier for him to take the medicine that way.'

John stared at his son for a heartbeat and then gently lifted him into his arms. He cradled his head before learning down to kiss him gently in his hair.

'Come on, boyo, you need to take some stuff to make you feel better.'

Jenny carefully measured out the liquid pain relief sachet that a passenger had provided and handed the small measuring cup to John, who held it to his son's lips.

'You'll like this, it's strawberry,' he said.

Sonia reappeared, and handed Jenny a small packet of jam before placing a fresh cloth on her son's head. Jenny watched as Tommy's parents exchanged glances, and wondered at what message had passed between them. She then carefully separated a capsule of antibiotic, tipped the contents onto a plastic spoon, and mixed it with jam.

Jenny felt movement behind her.

'Five hundred milligrams?' she asked Luc as he knelt beside her.

She watched as Luc appeared to make a quick calculation in his head.

'For now. We might need to up it for the next dose, but I don't want to push his other organs at the moment.'

Jenny nodded, handed the spoon to John, and watched as he coaxed Tommy to take the medicine. The look on Tommy's face told her that the jam had helped, but had not completely masked the foul taste of the vital antibiotics.

'We need to clean the wound,' Luc said, reaching into his bag for sterile gauze and a pair of gloves. 'No normal saline; not allowed to bring it on the plane.'

'I'll get some boiled water and salt. It's not ideal, but . . . ' She let the sentence hang in the air.

Luc nodded. 'It will have to do.'

Jenny watched as Luc expertly cleaned the wound. Tommy flinched and tried to move away, but his dad held him tightly and whispered soothing words. Sonia continued to almost mechanically mop the boy's forehead.

Luc finally placed an absorbent dressing over the top of the small wound that was making the boy so poorly.

'You alright to bandage?' Luc asked, looking directly at her as if he was truly seeing her for the first time. Jenny felt momentarily trapped in his gaze, and all power of speech left her. She nodded her head in affirmation.

'The captain says we should shortly be in range, so I should be able to radio through to the hospital in Atlanta.'

As he stood, he reached out and put a hand on her shoulder. Although it was the briefest of touches, Jenny felt as if it had left a mark. She shook off the feeling quickly, and turned her attention back to the job in hand. She gently and efficiently bandaged the now-cleaned wound, before elevating the boy's leg on one of the small airline pillows. Jenny then rechecked his blood pressure and pulse. Both parents looked at her, their eyes showing they were desperate for some good news.

'No change,' she said, with a

reassuring look, 'but that's good.'

She swiftly checked Tommy's temperature, running the wand across his forehead.

'Temperature is down a bit, which means the medication is helping. Hopefully he will get some sleep.'

Jenny felt a hand on her shoulder and looked up into Luc's face. With a slight gesture, he asked her to follow him.

'Blood pressure low but holding, pulse slightly increased. Temperature down to thirty-eight.' Jenny's report was short and succinct.

Luc nodded. 'All we can really do is try to prevent his condition worsening. I'd be happier if we had some IV fluids we could administer. Progression of shock is a real issue.'

'Do we have any rehydration sachets on board?' Jenny turned and asked Glen, who seemed to materialise whenever they needed something.

'I take that as a no,' Luc said, taking in the man's expression.

'Is the kid that sick?' Glen asked

Jenny and Luc exchanged glances. They both knew the answer to that, but neither of them were going to say it out loud.

'His condition is serious, but we will do all we can.'

'We can make a rehydration fluid. It's not ideal, but it might buy us some time,' Jenny said. Luc looked at her thoughtfully, and she breathed out the blush she could feel forming on her neck at being under his scrutiny.

'I'll have to look up the amounts, but good idea.'

Jenny turned to Glen. 'I need a litre of bottled water, and some sugar and salt.'

Glen bustled around the galley to find what she had asked for. Luc looked questioningly at her.

'Half a teaspoon of salt, and six of sugar, in a litre of water. I need the water boiled and still warm. I help out with the Scouts, we camp,' Jenny added with a shrug to Luc, who looked as if he was filing away this additional piece of information about her. She turned and started to make up the mixture.

'Put this in the fridge, and when it's cool enough to drink, bring it to us.'

* * *

Jenny glanced at her watch for what she knew was the millionth time.

'Another hour,' Luc said softly.

They were both sat perched on the edge of seats at the front of the plane's First Class lounge. Sonia and John were sat on the floor, their backs leaning against the compartment wall, with Tommy cradled across their laps.

'Let's see if we can get some more fluid into him,' Luc said, and Jenny knelt down and carefully poured some rehydration liquid onto the spoon.

'Tommy, love,' Sonia said softly, running her hand across the boy's forehead.

The boy lay still.

'Come on, son,' John murmured. 'I

know you're tired, but you need to drink. It will make you feel better.'

'Tommy?' Sonia's voice was high with anxiety.

Jenny reached out a hand and pinched the boy on his earlobe — the least painful way to test for a response — but there was nothing. Jenny felt Luc slide off his seat and kneel beside her as she pulled the stethoscope from round her neck and began to check his blood pressure. When she had finished she handed it to Luc who ran through checks of his own, first listening to Tommy's heart and then lungs. Jenny checked other vital signs.

'Blood pressure has dropped slightly, pulse one-ten, temperature thirty-eight-two.'

Jenny swallowed, knowing that Tommy's parents were both wide-eyed with fear. She forced herself to look at them as Luc spoke.

'Tommy's condition has worsened,' he said softly. 'But we are less than an hour away from Atlanta, where we can quickly get him the intensive care that he needs.'

'There must be something that you can do! You're a doctor, for God's sake!' John's voice was loud and cracked, and Jenny was aware that the rest of First Class — which had already been quiet — was now silent, as if all the other passengers were holding their breath.

From experience, Jenny knew the anger wasn't really directed at them. The fear of losing a loved one, especially a child, brought out the most basic terror in everyone and emotions inevitably ran high.

'We are doing what we can,' Luc said, his voice low-pitched and showing no signs of reaction to the angry outburst. 'I'm going to go and update Atlanta. We have an ambulance and team standing by at the airport.'

He looked at Jenny now, and the message was clear. There was nothing else he could do and they both knew that his presence, as the target of John's rage, would for the next few minutes only make things worse. He was going to leave her, but he would not be far away if the situation changed.

'It's okay. It's going to be okay,' John was whispering to his son, rocking him back and forth gently. Sonia was clutching onto one of Tommy's hands. Jenny reached out a hand for Sonia's arm, and was relieved when the other woman didn't shrink back at her touch. They looked at each other and Jenny could see a calmness return. Jenny nodded, and then picked up a fresh cloth to wipe Tommy's forehead and chest. She knew it would do little, but it was a comforting gesture, showing that she was at least doing something. It also meant that she could keep a watchful eye on Tommy's breathing rate, which would give her an early warning that his condition was deteriorating further.

'I don't understand why this is happening? Why him?' John looked up at Jenny, and she could remember all the times she had been asked that agonising question before.

'It's not your fault, John. Sometimes infections take hold in the shortest period of time and catch us out a little. We have started Tommy on antibiotics.'

John cut across her: 'Then why aren't they working?' There was no anger now, just pleading for an answer.

'Oral antibiotics can take time to take effect, but that doesn't mean they aren't working,' she said gently, knowing that what Tommy needed was fast-acting, powerful, intravenous antibiotics, plus fluids and intensive care support. 'When we land, the doctors can give Tommy much stronger drugs and fluids, as well as test for what bug is causing all the trouble. It's less than an hour now, and he will get the best care available.'

Jenny reached out and checked the boy's pulse. It was not really necessary at that moment, but she knew that Tommy's parents needed to see her do something, anything, which they could tell themselves was helping their son. Jenny knew that all they could really do was watch and wait and hope.

4

Luc and Jenny sat side by side on the floor. Despite the fact they were in First Class, there wasn't much room, so they were so close they almost touched. Jenny moved an inch, all too aware of Luc's presence next to her, and needing to put even the smallest amount of distance between them. Now they had done all they could for Tommy, the minutes dragged like hours, and to keep her mind from panicking she tried to let it wander. The problem was, the only thing her brain seemed capable of thinking of — apart from the current situation with Tommy — was the man sat next to her.

His calmness in a crisis told her that he was a doctor from a field similar to hers — emergency medicine, perhaps, or maybe intensive care. All doctors knew they must be calm in a crisis, of course, but the situation they were in was unusual even for doctors, and she knew that some would have been unable to hide their panic or concern as Luc had done. She risked a glance at him and realised that he was looking at her; or, perhaps more accurately, studying her. He smiled seemingly unconcerned at being caught staring. She couldn't quite master up the same level of bravado, and so looked away.

What was she doing even *thinking* about another man? That was not why she was here. She was getting away to get her head straight, to work out what she wanted to do with her life now that everything had changed. Having a schoolgirl crush on a man she had just met was definitely not part of the plan.

At that moment, the plane banked, and Jenny was caught unawares. As if the action was occurring in slow motion, she felt herself slide towards Luc with no means to stop herself. For his part, Luc seemed more aware of the movement of the plane, and reached

42

out an arm to prevent her falling into his lap. Instead, she found herself falling into his arms. The plane levelled off and she forced herself to sit up, even though every part of her had found surprising comfort in being held. Luc showed no desire to let her go, either.

'Sorry,' Jenny said, readjusting her position so that she could reach out for the arm of a nearby seat if the plane banked again.

'Not a problem,' Luc replied, and Jenny could see the light dance in his eyes before he turned his attention to check on Tommy.

'No change,' he said softly to the small group huddled around him. 'But that's good. He is holding his own, and we must be nearly there.'

At that moment Glen reappeared.

'We have been granted permission to land at Atlanta. They are holding other aircraft back to allow us to go first. We will need you to take your seats.'

Luc and Jenny stood up. Glen continued, addressing John and Sonia:

'I have asked two of our customers in First Class if they would mind taking your seats in the back so that you can remain here with your son, and near to Doctor Buchannan. I haven't been able to arrange a seat for you . . . ' Glen turned his attention to Jenny, who nodded. She had hoped to see Tommy off the plane, but it really only took one medical professional to hand over to the doctors on the ground, and Luc was eminently more qualified than she was.

'No problem,' she said, before turning to John and Sonia. 'Take care,' she told them, knowing that anything else would be a useless platitude.

Jenny turned to walk away but a hand prevented her.

'Thank you,' Sonia said, and then reached up to kiss her quickly on the cheek.

'I'm glad I was here to help,' Jenny replied with the reassuring smile that she had practiced over the years.

Jenny walked to the curtain that separated First Class from the galley area, and couldn't resist one last look. She watched as Luc carefully lifted Tommy in his arms whilst his parents found their seats and seatbelts. Glen stepped forward with more pillows and blankets, and Luc laid Tommy in his father's arms with such gentleness that Jenny could feel the tears that had been threatening start to build behind her eyes. It was always like this. During a crisis she was calm and in control but afterwards, it was as if all that emotion she had kept at bay needed a way out. With a deep breath she made her way back to her seat in Economy.

She was aware that eyes were on her now. She suspected that this was no longer because she was a source of curious sympathy, but because now they all wanted to know if the ill passenger was going to make it. Jenny fought to keep her face neutral, to not show her own fears for Tommy, and took her seat. There were muffled conversations now, but no longer about her and her missing husband, now the passengers' attention had been diverted to what had happened behind the curtains in First Class.

The seatbelt light came on with a ping, and Jenny found hers and clicked it together. The older lady sat next to the window nudged her husband, but he shook his head; Jenny suspected that they wanted to know what had happened, but the husband didn't want to ask. Not that Jenny would be able to tell them anything: just because they were on a plane didn't mean that the public had the right to know about the medical information of another. So she leaned back and closed her eyes. Which had to be a signal that a person did not want to speak about it, surely?

'Ladies and gentlemen, this is your captain speaking. We will shortly be landing at Hartsfield-Jackson Airport in Atlanta. We apologise for any inconvenience caused due to our diversion, but it has been necessary due to a passenger in urgent need of medical attention. When we land, please can I ask that you remain in your seats whilst the passenger is offloaded. Our cabin crew will be around with some complimentary drinks, and we hope to be on our way as soon as possible.'

Jenny kept her eyes firmly closed, knowing that if she opened them she would inevitably make eye contact with one of her fellow passengers, who would then no doubt want a full briefing on the current situation. She listened as the engine sound got louder, and felt herself pushed back into her seat as they hit the runway with a gentle bump.

'Here they come.' The older woman's voice sounded, and Jenny knew that she would have to look too. She needed to see that Tommy and his family were handed over to medical professionals with all the equipment and drugs that he needed so badly, so she turned her head and watched as the red lights of an American ambulance flashed across the tarmac. A truck with a huge ladder trailer also appeared, and was manoeuvred into position near the front of the plane and the doors which led to First Class.

The opening of the doors seemed to change the pressure in the cabin, and the fresh air outside made the curtains to the galley billow. Jenny didn't see Tommy until the paramedics had reached the bottom of the stairs, clicked the stretcher's wheeled legs into position, and started to wheel him towards the waiting ambulance. She could see Luc speaking to a man in scrubs, who was listening intently. Sonia and John jogged alongside their son. Jenny watched as Luc firmly closed the doors of the ambulance and banged on them to indicate to the driver that all were aboard. He stood there for a moment, shielding his eyes from the sun, and watched as the ambulance sped across the runway with lights continuing to flash.

When Luc turned, he glanced up towards the plane, and Jenny wondered for a moment if he was looking for her.

She shook her head at her own foolishness: she was sure he had forgotten all about her now. His thoughts had probably turned to the holiday that awaited him now the medical crisis was over.

'Ladies and gentlemen, we are awaiting our turn to take off, and so we shall shortly be resuming our flight to Grand Cayman. We have notified the authorities at that airport, so if any of you have onward flights from there, please be assured that alternative arrangements are being made.'

The announcement made Jenny sit up in her seat. She didn't have a connecting flight to worry about. Her destination was large enough to house an airport, but she knew from the itinerary the travel company had sent her that she needed to catch a small ferry, one that ran only twice a day. She had been booked on the morning journey. All she could do now was to hope that she would arrive in time for the afternoon ferry, or she was going to have to find somewhere to stay overnight, and she had a feeling she wouldn't be the only person looking for accommodation. She closed her eyes again and tried to breathe away the sense of rising panic. This was why she had only ever travelled to Spain and the Canary Islands. This was why Kai had teased her so much about being unadventurous. Maybe that was why he wasn't here beside her now, reassuring her and taking charge.

'You don't need him,' she told herself firmly. 'You are a grown woman. You manage a busy Emergency Department. You can do this!'

When the plane landed again, the jolt was much heavier, and Jenny started. She must have fallen asleep despite her anxiety. *Not an unusual reaction to a high-stress situation*, she told herself.

Her fellow passengers were shifting in their seats, and pulling luggage that they had managed to store under the seat in front into their laps. There was excited conversation now. Many of them had now arrived at their holiday destination, and were talking about how desperate they were for a swim and a cold drink. Jenny's sense of dread had only increased despite her nap. She now needed to navigate her way through Passport Control and Customs, and then find a taxi that would take her to the right ferry terminal. Just the thought of it made her shiver, but she knew she really didn't have a choice.

When the doors were opened and people started to file past, she stood up and recovered her bag from the overhead locker with some effort. It seemed that Jemima had ensured that her bag was right at the back of the bin, and she had to tell herself firmly to let it go, that it hadn't necessarily been done on purpose. She joined the queue and made her way down the steps to the tarmac, the hot, dry air blasting her face and making her auburn curls dance. If she had been thinking straight, she would have looked for her sunglasses — she knew they were in her bag somewhere — but she was suddenly overwhelmed with the image of her red silk knickers flying through the air, and decided that one thing she could do to avoid another embarrassing situation was wait until she could look carefully through her bag. Instead, she squinted and raised a hand to shade her eyes.

She made her way through Passport Control and Customs with ease, then found herself in a vast hall with hundreds of other people. Around the walls were men and women holding signs with names written on them. There were also holiday reps — wearing far too much make-up, in Jenny's opinion — in freshly-pressed uniforms. As Jenny's trip had been booked on the Internet, she knew there would be no one waiting for her with a warm, reassuring smile. She rearranged her carry-on to balance on top of her wheeled suitcase, and dragged it towards a door which had a picture of a car above it. She hoped this meant that she would find a taxi outside.

Outside was definitely where you waited if you wanted a taxi, judging by the sheer number of people gathered there. It was loud and colourful. Car horns beeped on the road that ran beside the front of the airport. People called and shouted to each other with an enthusiasm that Jenny was not used to, even though she lived in London. Airport buses drew up with the names of hotels on them, and people bustled through the crowds and climbed aboard. White and grey minivans pulled up, bearing the names of resorts and hotels. Drivers in brightly-coloured shirts stepped out and reeled off names before loading luggage into the back of the vans. Jenny stood and watched, not sure what else to do. Everyone in the crowd seemed to know what they were doing and where they were going.

The crowd started to thin, but Jenny had seen no sign of a taxicab that would be available for hire. She had found her sunglasses, and a spot to stand in that offered some shade, but she was still hot, and felt like her freckly skin was starting to burn.

A black car pulled up and honked its horn. Jenny looked on, wondering if she should go back into the airport and ask someone. The horn sounded again, and it seemed like no one was responding. Then the side slid open, and Jenny didn't think she had ever been so pleased to see a friendly face.

'Jenny!' Luc's face appeared above the crowd. 'Do you need a lift?' He waved his hand in the air, not sure if he had got her attention. She nodded gratefully, and felt like she might cry again — but this time with relief.

'Ladies and gents, please can I ask you to make room for the lovely lady . . . ' Luc had been joined by the taxi driver, who sported a broad grin. He gestured at the crowd, which parted for her, and she made her way to the vehicle. The driver opened the boot and she attempted to lift up her case.

'No, no, darling. You leave that to me.

That's my job, see.' Jenny smiled with relief. Finally, someone who was willing to help her out.

'Thank you,' she said, but she was waved off. Luc held open the door for her, and she slid into the back seat of the — thankfully — air-conditioned car.

'Here,' Luc said, 'you look like you need this. Important to keep hydrated out here.'

Jenny took the chilled bottle of water from him as if it were the most expensive champagne, and started to drink, ignoring the fact that a bead of water was running down her chin. She only stopped when Luc laughed; suddenly self-conscious, she wiped a hand across her face to pick up any drips.

'So, where are you headed, Nurse Jenny?' the taxi driver asked as he started the engine. Jenny blinked in surprise and was rewarded with a roar of laughter from the front seat.

'Doctor Luc hasn't stopped talking about you.'

Jenny raised an eyebrow and looked at Luc, who just shrugged.

'It was a fairly eventful flight,' he said with a grin. Jenny smiled back.

'It was. Have you heard anything?'

'Only that our suspicions were right. Toxic shock, probably a staph infection. He's getting all the right treatment, but only time will tell.'

Jenny digested this information. It really was all they could have hoped for at this stage.

'If you give me your contact details, I can let you know. If you like?' Luc made a gesture as if it didn't matter to him one way or the other, but Jenny felt a warm glow start in her heart and make its way down to her stomach. It was a very pleasant sensation, and not one she had felt for some time.

'I'd really like to know how Tommy does,' Jenny said carefully, not wanting to give away any indication of the impact of Luc's words. 'Not sure if my mobile will work here, though,' she said, before reaching into her hand luggage and searching for it. She froze when she heard a snort of laughter from the driver, and looked up just in time to see an exchange of looks between the two men. She felt the all-too-familiar burn of embarrassment. Clearly, Luc had told the driver *everything* about her.

'I'm never going to live that one down, am I?' Jenny mumbled out loud to no one in particular.

'Sorry,' Luc said, and he did at least look slightly abashed. 'It's such a good story, I couldn't resist. Armand didn't believe me, of course.'

Jenny looked up to the rear-view mirror and could see Armand was watching her.

'Well, Armand, I can assure you that particularly mortifying moment did, in fact, happen.'

Armand grinned back, and Jenny couldn't help but laugh. It was funny, even if it hadn't felt like it at the time, and besides she ought to be used to it. Those sorts of toe-curling incidents seemed to be a regular occurrence in her life. And it had to be better to laugh about them than sulk.

'Well, Nurse Jenny with the red knickers, where do I have the pleasure of taking you today?'

Jenny shook her head at the name, but her grin remained firmly in place. She was sure it was the relief of being around people who seemed to care, even if they had only just met. Maybe this travelling alone thing wasn't something to be afraid of after all!

'I need to catch a ferry to St. Emilie, so the ferry terminal or port thingy,' she said, knowing herself that she was being ridiculously vague and that she really ought to know where she was going.

There was another exchange of looks.

'What?' she asked, wondering if she was about to be told that that particular island was not a safe place for a single female traveller to go.

'You're in luck, Nurse Jenny. We are headed there too. Catching the last ferry back home.'

Jenny sank back in her seat a little. She felt as if she had been well and truly rescued. It was a slightly strange feeling. One of the reasons she only ever travelled in Europe was that she liked to feel like she was in control and knew what she was doing. This trip was so far outside of her comfort zone that she couldn't help but feel relieved.

'So, holidaying on St. Emilie?' Luc asked. 'We don't get that many tourists since it's off the beaten track.'

'We?' she asked.

'Doctor Luc is a local,' Armand said.

Jenny looked slightly puzzled, since although Luc had an accent which she couldn't place, it didn't sound anything like the up-and-down-ness of Armand's.

'Born in Glasgow,' Luc said, 'but raised on St. Emilie. My mum was born here. She came over to attend medical school in Edinburgh. Met my dad, who was a local. They moved back over here when my brother was born.'

A shadow passed across Luc's face, and Jenny again looked at the rear-view mirror. Armand's face registered sadness, but he quickly looked away.

'Anyway,' Luc said, his smile returning, 'that's my potted history. What's yours? Do you usually travel to far-off places all by yourself?' The look on Luc's face told her that he doubted that last very much, and Jenny felt a lurch in her stomach at the idea of telling someone else about the disaster that was her life.

5

'I'm sort of on my honeymoon,' she said wincing at how ridiculous that sounded now she had said it out loud. There was really no other way to put it.

'Isn't it usual to go on honeymoon with your new husband or wife?' Luc asked.

Jenny sighed. Knowing what had happened to you was bad, but having to tell others was even worse.

'I believe that is the norm,' she said, and then shook her head at what had seemed like a good idea at the time. 'My fiancé decided on Monday that he didn't want to marry me.' She surprised herself by being able to say it in a matter-of-fact way. The silence in the car was deafening. But Jenny was getting used to that response. Most people didn't know what to say to that kind of announcement.

'Wow, that's rough. I'm really sorry, Jenny.' Luc looked so sincere, no trace of amusement now, that Jenny thought she might lose control and cry . . . and maybe fall into his arms. She gave herself a little shake.

'It's fine, really,' she said in what had become a well-rehearsed response. 'Better to find out now than later.' A well-meaning aunt had greeted her news with this statement and Jenny had latched onto it, even though it did nothing to stem the flow of pain that resulted every time she thought about Kai.

'I'm not sure I could be so calm and collected about it,' Luc said, turning to gaze out of the window; for which Jenny was grateful, as it gave her the chance to wipe away a stray tear that had somehow escaped her control.

'Well if there's a place on earth that is so beautiful it can mend a broken heart, it's St. Emilie,' Armand said, glancing in his rear-view mirror and giving her an encouraging smile. Jenny managed to return it with one of her own.

'To be honest, I just had to get away from all the sympathy.'

Luc turned to look at her, and she felt she needed to explain herself.

'I know everyone means well, but with my friends and family it was like looking in a mirror at my own pain. I just needed some space, and since Kai — ' Her voice cracked on saying his name out loud, but she swallowed the lump that had suddenly formed, and forced herself to continue. ' — decided that he was going to go backpacking instead of getting married, I thought: why waste a perfectly good holiday?'

'Sounds like a plan, but I'm surprised you didn't bring a friend with you,' Luc said.

Jenny shrugged. 'Unfortunately, none of them could get three weeks off with only a few days' notice, so I didn't really have much choice. And besides, it will give me space, and time to read and think and . . . ' Jenny's voice trailed off as she realised she had given little thought to what she would do with herself for three weeks. All of her focus and energy had been aimed simply on getting here. She frowned to herself.

'Don't worry, you will find plenty to do, and most of it is relaxing,' Armand said. 'You know what I mean? Drinks looking out at the ocean, chillin' tunes, and friendly people. You'll be fine.'

Luc seemed to be lost in thought, and so Jenny turned to gaze out of the window as the car travelled along a road that was dusty, but lined with trees and plants that were the most vibrant shades of green she had ever seen. Children dressed in uniforms ran from a wooden building which Jenny assumed was a school. They laughed and joked and seemed to have no cares. Jenny could only long to feel that free.

'Where are you staying?' Luc's voice came out of the silence and Jenny jumped a little.

'Not really sure,' Jenny said ruefully.

'Don't worry, we can find you

somewhere. My sister runs a bar on the beach, she has a room that would probably do,' Armand said.

'No, I mean I *do* have somewhere to stay, but I don't really know much about it. Kai made all the arrangements.'

Jenny reached for the computer printout which listed all the information from Kai's various bookings.

'Er . . . 'La Cabane',' Jenny said wincing at her own pronunciation which she was sure was wrong.

Armand burst into laughter, and Jenny couldn't work out if it was her poor attempt at French or the place itself that had caused the response.

'I know, my French is terrible . . . ' she said, almost hopefully. Surely her luck could not be so bad as to have terrible accommodation for three weeks. Luc gasped as he tried to stop laughing.

'Sorry,' he said, catching a glimpse of her expression. '*La cabane* is French for 'shack'. Old Marcel discovered the

Internet a few years ago, and since then has been making a fortune from unsuspecting tourists who want an authentic experience of St. Emilie.'

Jenny stared, wide-eyed with impending gloom. This was so typical of Kai, who did everything he could to have a 'real' experience — which Jenny had recently come to understand actually meant 'as cheap as possible'. The only part of the wedding he had made any financial contribution to was the honeymoon, which he had insisted on organising, and now she suspected that she knew why. Jenny had to resist the urge to put her head in her hands, and instead rubbed her eyes, which now felt tired and gritty.

'It's really not that bad,' Luc said, clearly suddenly realising that joking with a recently-jilted bride might not be the best thing. 'It's basic, but functional. If you have any issues, we'll get Marcel to fix it or find you somewhere better to stay.' His words had come out in a tumble, and Jenny was surprised. It suddenly felt like she was being rescued in a way that she wasn't entirely comfortable with. Kai had always made her feel like she wouldn't be able to cope without him, as if her life was so sheltered that she couldn't deal with things. But that wasn't true, and she was going to prove it to herself on this trip.

'Thanks, but I'm sure I will be fine,' she said firmly. 'If there are any issues, I will speak to Marcel myself,' she added, to ensure that Luc understood all of her meaning. When she was sure that she had adopted an expression that indicated she meant every word, she turned to look at him, and was taken aback by the look of pain on his face. She opened her mouth to speak, wondering if her words had come out more sternly than she intended, but Luc had turned his head away from her. His body language screamed out that he did not want to talk anymore.

Jenny frowned in confusion. She looked towards Armand, and saw him shrug his shoulders, as if to say, *That's just Luc*. Jenny suddenly wished she had found her own taxi, made her own way to the ferry. She had been relieved at first, but now she was stuck in a car with someone who clearly didn't want her around anymore, and she'd had enough of that sensation just recently to last a lifetime.

When they arrived at the ferry terminal, Jenny had hoped she might lose herself in the crowds boarding the vessel, but her shoulders slumped when she took in the sight. In front of her was a small platform ferry, with room for a maximum of four cars or small trucks. There was a wheelhouse at one end, and a veranda-type area for the passengers who did not want to sit in the sun. Armand drove the car up the ramp and tucked in behind a small truck which had advertising for beer and soft drinks emblazoned on the side. There were a small number of people sat on the long line of weathered seats in the shade, and Jenny knew that she would have to stay with Luc and Armand at least until they got to St. Emilie.

Armand got out of the taxi and pulled open her door before she had the chance to open it for herself. He bobbed his head at her and she smiled. She knew her emotions were raw and close to the surface — perhaps she had overreacted. She followed Armand to the covered seating area, aware that Luc was following behind, but not quite ready to look at him yet. Armand gestured for her to take a seat.

'Can I get you something to eat?' Armand asked. 'The ferry takes a couple of hours, and that's if the weather is okay and the captain is in a good mood.' He smiled at her. 'You must be hungry by now,' he added, appearing to know that she was going to shake her head. 'Come on, now, that airline food is the worst.'

Jenny felt around in her bag for her purse. She had at least had the foresight to get some Grand Cayman dollars from the currency exchange at Heathrow. She had no idea how much food might cost, so she just picked out a couple of orange-coloured notes, surprised to notice that they had the image of the Queen just like the English money she also had in her purse.

'No, no, put it away. I didn't offer so you could pay. You like chicken?'

Jenny nodded uncertainly. She knew enough to be careful about what she ate in exotic places, and she couldn't see where a kitchen could be on the ferry.

'Relax, the food is good here. Therese cooks it all.' Luc gestured a hand to the barbeque set up at the back of the deck. 'It tastes good, and it's always fresh. So no need to worry.'

Jenny nodded and risked a glance in his direction. The sudden mood change in the car had gone, and Luc's face was relaxed and open. For a moment she wondered if she had imagined the whole thing. Perhaps she had fallen asleep and dreamt it.

'It can get a little rough once we are

out in open water, so I hope you have better sea legs than me.'

Jenny reached into her bag and pulled out a small cardboard box of travel pills.

'I came prepared. Do you want some?'

'Nah, I think I'll tough it out. Those things make me drowsy, and it looks pretty calm.'

Those, thought Jenny an hour later, *were famous last words.*

6

The weather had hit as they rounded the point. The waves increased in tempo from a gentle lapping to tossing the ferry about like a toy boat in a bathtub. The other passengers seemed unfazed, and simply planted their feet wide apart on the deck and held on. Jenny decided that this must be a sign that this sort of crossing was not unusual, and therefore nothing to worry about. She gave thanks to the pharmaceutical gods that she had taken the pills, or she felt sure she would be joining Luc at the rail disposing of the delicious grilled chicken they had all eaten.

'He's forgotten what it's like. Been away too long,' Armand said. 'Lost his sea legs.'

'How long has it been?' Jenny asked, thinking that whilst she had faith in the pills, a distracting conversation might also help her stomach.

'He left for university when he was eighteen. Came back in the summer sometimes, but this will be the first time he's been home for any length of time. We're all starting to forget what he looks like!'

'He's not back for a holiday, then?' Jenny asked, now curious.

'Oh, no, he's following in his mother's footsteps. He's taking over the clinic.'

Jenny sat back and thought about this. 'Why now, I wonder?' She realised she had spoken the words out loud.

'I think that's something you should ask him,' Armand said, nodding his head in the direction of Luc's back.

'Of course,' Jenny said. 'Sorry. Just thinking out loud.'

Armand nodded, as if to say *That's alright*, and they both watched as another wave of sickness overcame Luc and made him lean back over the side.

'Perhaps I should check on him

again,' Jenny said.

'You don't know much about men, do you?'

Jenny turned to Armand, but was relieved to see he was smiling.

'Girl, no man likes to be seen in such a sorry state, particularly when the girl is as pretty as you.'

Jenny laughed, but could feel the colour rise in her cheeks.

'And besides, he didn't eat that much chicken. He'll be done soon.'

Luc finally retook his seat beside Jenny, and now it was her turn to offer him a bottle of water. Luc regarded it with a pained expression, clearly weighing up whether a sip would result in more sickness.

'You need to keep hydrated,' Jenny said, unable to hide her smile as she remembered how he had used the exact same words on her. Luc grimaced, but accepted the bottle and took a tentative sip. The ferry rolled again and some spray washed over the side, breaking on the top of the beer truck. Luc groaned.

Jenny reached in her bag for a tissue, wetted it with water from her own bottle, and handed it to him.

'Back of the neck,' she said. 'It helps, trust me.'

Luc lifted the wet tissue to the back of his neck and leaned back in his seat.

'Not something they teach in medical school.'

'Nope, but fortunately for you I didn't go to medical school, and if there's one thing that nurses know how to deal with, it's vomiting patients.'

Luc winced at the word, but Jenny thought that his face looked slightly less green.

'I'm glad you're here to help me. Again.'

Jenny shrugged.

'You did most of the work.'

'You kept Tommy — and, more importantly, his parents — calm. There wasn't much we could actually do, but I know that helped.'

Jenny decided to accept the compliment — not something she found easy.

'Thank you,' she said, softly.

'Not the best way to start your holiday, though,' he said thoughtfully.

'Firstly, it's my *honeymoon*, remember?' He looked at her and she laughed. 'Well, it is. Obviously minus the husband. When you're faced with honeymooning alone, a medical emergency on your flight over doesn't seem so bad.'

Luc managed a small burst of laughter before his stomach demanded his attention once more. He held a hand to his mouth, and Jenny could see him try and take some slow deep breaths to fend off the nausea.

'Any news?' she asked, thinking that might distract him.

He felt in his pocket for his mobile and pulled it out. 'No signal. Not much of one on the island unless you're near the main town, but hopefully any messages will come in once we reach port.'

He leaned forward and clasped his hands in front of him.

76

'If I live that long,' he added, with a moan. Jenny reached out a hand instinctively for his back, paused for a moment. It was such a natural response for a nurse to offer touch as a kind of comfort, but she wasn't sure how it would be received and she also wasn't sure how it would make her feel. As always, her nursing instinct kicked in and she placed a hand on the small of his back and rubbed it gently. Some of the tension from Luc's shoulders seemed to dissolve and after a few more deep breaths he sat back in his chair, before taking another sip of water.

* * *

By the time the small island appeared on the horizon, Jenny had to admit that she was ready to get off the boat almost as much as Luc. The expression 'rolling seas' had found new meaning in the crossing from Grand Cayman to St. Emilie. Their fellow passengers either seemed resigned to it, or had had plenty of practice at coping with the listing and rollercoaster motion of the ferry. Her stomach had started to send warning signals to her brain, but Jenny ignored them, and kept reminding herself that she had taken the pills and so was not going to be sick.

A few people moved to the front of the ferry, and Jenny watched them go.

'Come on,' Luc said with a groan, 'you have to come and see the best view of the island.'

He lurched a little, and Jenny instinctively held out an arm. She was rewarded with a smile.

'Don't worry, I think I can stagger that far.'

They moved slowly, trying to predict the pitch of the boat with each step, but finally made it to the railings. The sight took Jenny's breath away. The rolling seas gave the impression of poor weather, but St. Emilie was like an oasis in the storm. It seemed to be backlit with pure, brilliant sunshine, which made the waves lapping on the stretch of golden beach sparkle.

'It looks like paradise,' Jenny whispered. Luc grinned, and another passenger who stood nearby said, 'That it is, girl, that it is. Welcome to St. Emilie.' The older man threw his arms wide as if he were personally inviting her to his private island.

'Just keep it to yourself, mind,' he added with mock sternness. 'We don't want everybody finding out.'

'This is the south end: has beautiful beaches, but it bears the brunt of any bad weather. The port is round on the west side, where most people live.'

Jenny nodded, but couldn't tear her eyes away from the view. For the first time since Kai had announced he didn't want to marry her, she felt something nearing affection for him. He had picked a truly magical place.

* * *

As with most things to do with Kai, the magical feeling didn't last very long.

Armand pulled the car up to stop on a road which had a light dusting of sand and ran parallel to the beach. Jenny had almost missed her accommodation, assuming it was someone's shed. It was a wooden shack that leaned to one side. The roof had been patched with assorted objects, one of which looked like a metal road sign.

'Well, this is it,' Luc said, and Jenny knew he was watching closely for her reaction. Remembering the cross words they had shared earlier that day, she forced a smile onto her face.

'Well, you were right — it definitely is authentic.'

Armand grunted.

'Only if you go back fifty years. No true islander has lived in something like that for decades.' He turned to her now.

'You don't have to stay here, you know. I can have a word with my sister. She'd be happy to put you up.'

'I'm sure it will be fine, thanks,' Jenny said, knowing that what she had come to the island for was some time away from other people, and an opportunity to think about what she wanted to do with her life.

'Okay, but if you change your mind . . . ' Armand said as he stepped out of the driver's seat and pulled her suitcase from the boot of the car. 'My sister owns a bar in town, about ten minutes' walk up the road. Just keep following it, but if you get lost, ask for Francie's. Everyone round here knows everyone else.'

Armand made to carry the suitcase to the front of the hut.

'I can manage, thanks,' she said, taking hold of the suitcase. 'Do you know where I get the key?' she added, suddenly realising yet another thing she should have found out before she left.

Armand laughed. 'There's no key, girl. Nobody locks their doors round here; and besides, if you tried to fix a lock to that door, the whole place would fall over.' He exchanged a look with Luc, who had remained in the car but was looking out of the window.

'We'll all be at Francie's later for supper, if you feel like joining us?' Luc said. 'No pressure,' he added quickly, seeing the look on Jenny's face. All she wanted right now was a shower and a nap, and not necessarily in that order.

'Or wait till breakfast,' Armand said. 'We eat there all the time. Best place to find us,' he added, and slammed the boot closed.

'Then I will definitely see you at some point,' Jenny said, 'although maybe not for supper, I'm thinking I might just go straight to bed.'

Both Armand and Luc nodded, and then the car disappeared up the road. Jenny could now truly take in her surroundings. There were no other buildings around, just a mixture of wind-bent trees and bushes that lined the road. Through them, she could see the beach beyond, and the sea.

'Well, you wanted peace and quiet and to be away from everything. Looks like you got it,' she told herself, and started to drag her heavy suitcase across the sand to her new home.

She had to walk around the building twice before she could work out which bit of wood functioned as the front door. The door seemed stuck, and Jenny briefly wondered if there was in fact a lock and a key, but with some careful wriggling of the handle and some shoving with her whole body weight she managed to force the door open, scraping it across the wooden floor. The inside of the hut was no more promising than the outside. Against one wall was a rickety bed frame that looked as if it had once been painted white. The bedlinen looked old, but seemed clean. Around the room were higgledy-piggledy mismatched shelves and furniture. The pots and pans for the kitchen hung off nails in the wall. There was a rusted fridge — which, thankfully, appeared to be working, and had a few bottles of water in it — and an old wood-burning stove. A curtain hung over a doorway to what was the bathroom: a drain in the floor, a shower head that dripped, and a toilet.

Jenny returned to the main room and threw herself on the bed. There would certainly be no distractions here. There was no TV; but she scanned the shelves, which were cluttered with mismatched china and assorted ornaments, and her eyes fell on an old transistor radio. She heaved herself off the bed and went to switch it on. At first, all she could hear was crackling and interference, but with a few adjustments to the only button she found a station that was playing the relaxed music of the Caribbean.

Jenny flipped her suitcase open and started to unpack. Once she had a few familiar things around her, she felt less like she was a million miles from home and all alone. She yawned as a wave of tiredness hit. Plonking the suitcase in front of the door to act as a warning in case she had any uninvited guests, she returned to the bed, falling asleep within minutes, listening to the sound of the sea hitting the beach.

7

The crash woke her, and for a moment Jenny had no idea where she was. The room she was in was so dark that she couldn't make out anything about it. She reached out blindly, hoping to find her mobile phone or a lamp that might let her see better, but located nothing. There was another crash, though this one sounded far away; a boom; and then the room she was in was lit up as if someone had started a very large fire. The few moments of light allowed Jenny to process her surroundings. She was in the hut on the beach, in the Caribbean, supposedly on her honeymoon. There was another flash of light, and Jenny could now place the disturbance — thunder and lightning. She slid out of her bed, made her way over to the light's pull-cord, and tugged on it. Nothing happened, and with the fading lightning she was plunged back into darkness.

She stood still, too unfamiliar with her surroundings to feel safe to walk around and not bump into something. Force of habit made her count the seconds that passed between the next rumble of thunder and flash of lightning. Only three seconds. The storm was well and truly close. She couldn't quite believe she had managed to sleep through it to this point. Each flash of light allowed her to pinpoint things that she needed. She found her small carry-on bag and dug out her phone. There was no signal, but at least the battery was still charged, and so she used the flashlight function to look through the cupboards. She found a couple of candles, and another search led her to a discarded lighter. She lit the candles and stood them on plates around the room.

Her phone told her it was three-twenty so she knew that she had slept through supper — not that she would even consider going out in this weather. The wind dropped suddenly and another sound caught her ears. She shook herself; it was probably just an animal out and about. The noise persisted, and Jenny knew that she couldn't ignore it. On the back of the front door was a nail on which was hooked an old fisherman's yellow jacket. She pulled it on; it was far too big, so covered her up well past her knees. She had found no other torch in her search, and when she opened the door, the sudden gust of wind blew out all the candles.

The cry came again, and so she held her phone out in front of her and tried to peer into the total blackness. The sensible part of her was telling her that she was being foolish. No one would be out in this, and any wildlife would almost certainly have found shelter. It was probably just the wind. Promising herself she would walk around the hut once, check out the road, and then go back inside and relight the candles, she stepped carefully out into the storm.

The wind was so fierce that it defeated any attempts to keep her hood up. The rain fell like a waterfall, and soon her hair was soaked and clinging to her head. As she made her way around the hut, she thought she could see an intermittent flash of light. Squinting, she walked towards what she thought was the source. Another flash of lightning, and Jenny could see everything. A Jeep lay on its side, the headlights blinking on and off occasionally, and the sound — which Jenny was now sure was a human cry — was coming from nearby. The road was strewn with tree branches and palms, and it was difficult to pick her way over by only the light of her phone.

'Hello?' she shouted into the wind, but she doubted that it had carried it any distance.

Something brushed against Jenny's leg and she let out a scream. Covering her mouth with one hand, she forced herself to look down, and saw a small hand reaching out for her. She knelt down quickly, moving smaller branches that had formed a sort of cocoon around a young boy who couldn't be more than four years old. His eyes were wide and he was making a noise similar to an animal in pain. Jenny reached out for him, but he pulled himself into an even tighter ball.

'It's okay,' Jenny said softly. 'It's okay. I'm going to help you.'

As if that was the signal he needed, the boy threw himself into her arms and she held him tight.

'Does anything hurt?' Jenny had to shout to hear herself over the wind.

The boy didn't respond, so she carefully ran her hands over him, starting at his head. He had a nasty gash on his forehead, which was bleeding heavily, but nothing else felt immediately wrong. Jenny pulled up the fisherman's coat and felt for the bottom edge of her cotton blouse before tearing off a strip. Carefully, she tied the makeshift bandage around the boy's head. It was not ideal, but hopefully it would slow the bleeding until she could get him more help.

The boy was staring at the Jeep, and so Jenny stood and moved towards it, the boy holding her tightly by her legs. She leant down and lifted him into her arms so she could move more quickly, but also so that she could shield him from whatever she might find when she got there.

The Jeep lay on its side, and Jenny could smell fuel. The engine was thankfully silent, so fire was not an immediate concern. She leaned down and gently put the boy on the ground, but he clung on to her, and so she kept one arm firmly around his shoulders. Peering through the windscreen, she could make out a shadow, big enough to be a person.

'Hello? Can you hear me?'

Jenny turned her head into the wind and strained to hear a response, but there was none. She lifted the boy again, and made her way around to the side which was facing upwards.

'I need to try and open the door,' she said to the boy, who stared at her but loosened his grip a little. Jenny felt for the handle and pulled as hard as she could, but she didn't have the height to open the door.

'Stay here. I will be right back.' The boy whimpered, but seemed to understand as he released her leg and pulled his knees up to his chin. Jenny made her way around the back of the car and, using the tyre and rear bumper, pulled herself up so she was crouched on top of it.

Her canvas shoes fought to keep a grip on the slippery surface, but she managed to slide her way across to the door. She wedged one foot against the wing mirror and tried the door again. She managed to open it a crack, but a gust of wind slammed it shut and she lost her balance, falling hard against the wing mirror.

She felt a flash of pain register for a brief moment, but it was quickly gone

— no doubt washed away by the adrenaline that she could feel coursing through her. With a grunt of effort, she managed to pull the door open just wide enough for her to slide through and into the overturned Jeep.

She felt for the dashboard, so that she had something to rest her feet on, and steadied herself.

'Hello,' she tried again. Now she was shielded from the weather outside, her voice sounded loud and seemed to echo around the inside of the vehicle. This time, she was sure she heard a murmured moan.

'I'm Jenny. I'm here to help you. Can you tell me where you are hurt?'

'Taavi?' the voice said, which Jenny was certain was male, deep and full.

'Is that your son?' Jenny asked as she repositioned herself so that she could feel for a pulse.

'My boy . . .'

'He's okay. He has a cut to his head, but otherwise he seems fine. He's safe, he's outside.'

Jenny reached out a hand in the blackness to try and work out how the man was lying. Carefully, she felt around his head.

'Do you have any pain in your neck or back?' she asked.

'Pain everywhere.' The voice sounded as if it were being forced between clenched teeth.

Jenny reached for her pocket and pulled out the phone. The warning light was flashing now, indicating that she was nearly out of battery. She lifted it high and did a quick visual check. The man had a cut to his head too. There was also blood on the windscreen, and Jenny winced — clearly, the Jeep had no airbag. She felt the man's chest, and heard him take a sharp breath in.

'Sorry,' she said. 'I think you may have broken a few ribs. Can you wiggle your toes for me?'

She shone the light into the well of the car. She could just make out the movement of his feet, but more worrying was the pool of dark liquid which seemed likely to be blood. Leaning forward, she could see that the man's right leg had a long jagged cut that was bleeding profusely.

She shone her phone over the back seat and saw a sports bag. She wiggled in between the two front seats and pulled the bag into her lap. There was an assortment of clothes and towels inside. Quickly, she rolled the towel, and used it to carefully support the man's head in position.

'What's your name?' she asked as she worked.

'Salomen. Help my boy,' he said, turning to fix Jenny with his gaze.

'I have, and I will,' she said, 'but I need you to stay still. I'm not sure if you have hurt your back and neck, so you need to keep as still as possible.'

She pulled a t-shirt from the bag, and quickly fashioned it into a bandage for the wound on Salomen's leg.

'Salomen, I'm going to need to go for help. I won't be able to get you out of the car safely alone.'

Jenny lifted the light so that she could see his face. His eyes told her that he understood.

'Take my son,' he said.

'I will, and I'll be back with help as soon as I can. I promise.'

For a moment, Jenny couldn't make her limbs obey her. She didn't want to leave Salomen, although she knew she had no real choice. She would need help to get him out of the car; trying to move him on her own could make his injuries worse. She had no way to get him the assistance that he desperately needed without leaving him; but the truth was, she had no real idea where to go for this. All she could do was follow the road as Armand had told her, and hope that she came across someone or somewhere with a phone.

'I'll be back as soon as I can,' she said again; and then, knowing there was nothing else she could do, she levered herself back out through the door and climbed down to the ground.

Taavi was where she had left him. He

was curled up into a ball and rocking slightly. He jumped when she reached out a hand for him and pulled him up to his feet. She tugged gently on his hand, but he refused to move. She knelt down in front of him. She knew she could carry him if she had to, but that they would move more quickly — and therefore get help more quickly — if she could persuade him to walk.

'Taavi. I know you're scared, and I know you don't want to leave your dad, but he wants you to come with me.'

The little boy shook his head, and Jenny wasn't sure whether there were tears rolling down his face mixing with the raindrops.

'You dad is stuck in the Jeep, Taavi, and we need to go and get some help to get him out. Do you understand?' she added, feeling rather helpless and wondering if the boy's shock was worse than her initial assessment.

Suddenly the small hand in hers tightened its grip, and now she found herself being dragged forward. Of course the boy would know where to go for the nearest help. She ordered her shaking legs to obey her and started to run.

The storm raged on and it was difficult to see. Twice, they fell over tree limbs and other debris in the road. They ran on, and Jenny's side reminded her that she had fallen awkwardly, but she pushed back the discomfort and kept running. They reached the bar before she realised. The electricity was out here, too. There was a raised wooden platform on the beach with a palm-tree covering to give shade from the sun. There were no chairs or tables, but Jenny suspected they had been removed for safety. The only light was dim behind the window, and so Jenny rushed to it and started to hammer on the door. Taavi stood beside her, and she could feel that he was shaking, so she lifted him up into her arms and rubbed his back. They were both wet through and cold.

There was a creaking noise, and the

door to the bar was pulled open. Jenny didn't think she had ever been happier to see someone.

'Jenny? Girl, what you doing out in this weather?' Armand's face was just about visible in the light from his torch. He shone it towards them, and noticed the boy cradled in her arms. 'Is that Taavi? Where's your dad?'

'Accident,' Jenny said, suddenly finding that she was out of breath. 'His dad is trapped in the Jeep. He's hurt and trapped.'

Armand's eyes went wide, and then he turned on his heel and started yelling instructions. A woman stepped out: from her similar appearance to Armand, Jenny was certain this was Francie.

'Come inside,' she said, beckoning to Jenny. Gently, she lifted the boy from her arms and wrapped him in a blanket. 'Jocelyn, fetch the first aid kit and then make some tea. They're frozen.'

Jenny watched as the teenage girl opened a cupboard and pulled out a tin box before handing it to Jenny with a nod.

'You up to cleaning his wound?' Francie said. 'I can do it, but I'm no nurse.'

'I'm fine,' Jenny said. 'Really,' she added when she saw the look on Francie's face. 'I'm just a bit cold.'

Jenny tugged out a wrapped alcohol wipe and cleaned her hands before pulling on a set of gloves and turning her attention to her patient. 'Taavi, I need to clean this, okay?'

Taavi was still wide-eyed, but he nodded. Francie sat down beside him and put her arm around his shoulder, and the boy relaxed into the hug.

'There now,' Francie said. 'Your auntie will take good care of you, and Armand is going to go and fetch your dad.'

Jenny worked quickly, and was pleased to see the wound had stopped bleeding. It needed some glue to hold the wound edges together, but there was none in the otherwise well-stocked first aid kit, and she knew that the clinic where Luc worked was bound to have some.

'We're going to need some surgical glue, from the clinic,' Jenny said.

'Don't worry, child, we've sent for Doctor Luc. I can finish fixing up Taavi when we've seen to his dad.'

Armand reappeared holding some blankets and a crowbar.

'I'd best be taking the kit, if you've finished?' he asked Jenny.

'I'm done here for now. I'll bring it,' Jenny answered.

Armand looked uncertain.

'I'm coming too,' Jenny said, thinking that surely that must be obvious.

The front door opened, and a rush of wind and noise momentarily filled the room before it was firmly closed.

'Oh, no, you're not,' a familiar voice said.

8

Jenny turned and saw Luc standing in the doorway, framed by the light of the torch he held in his hand, giving the effect of a halo of light.

'I need to show you where Salomen is, and I can help.'

'No one is doubting that,' Luc said, putting down the large square rucksack which Jenny recognised as holding emergency medical equipment. 'But you're injured.' He gestured at Jenny, and with a frown she looked down and took in her bare legs, which were streaked with blood from the many cuts and scratches she had sustained in her short journey.

'They're superficial,' she said with a wave of her hand. 'I can sort myself out later.'

'You can sort yourself out now, and I'll take a look once we have rescued

Salomen. The risk of infection in this part of the world is much higher than in the UK.' He knelt down and pulled out some bandages, gauze, antiseptic solution and a tube of ointment that Jenny recognised as antibiotic. He walked over and placed them on one of the tables. 'Besides, the police are going to meet us there — the station is next door to the clinic,' he added in answer to her unasked question. 'We have all the help we need. Ready?'

Armand was by Luc's side, and he smiled at Jenny.

'You done the hardest bit, girl, now let the rest of us sort it out.'

Jenny opened her mouth to argue some more, but Luc had turned his back, clearly thinking that this was the way to win the argument. She made to take a step, but found a hand on her shoulder.

'Come,' said Francie, 'sit down; we'll sort out your legs, and you can have a cup of tea to warm you up.' Jenny found herself enveloped in a blanket and guided towards a chair and when she looked round, Armand and Luc were gone, back out into the storm, closing the door firmly behind them. As soon as she sat down, Jenny knew the effects of adrenaline were wearing off; she started to shake and fatigue was washing over her in waves.

'Here,' Jocelyn said handing her a cup of tea. When she realised that Jenny was shaking she used her own hands to support the cup so that Jenny could take a sip.

'Thanks,' Jenny said putting the cup on the table so that she wouldn't spill any of the contents. Jocelyn smiled and turned her attention to Taavi who seemed to have brightened up a little since he had had something to eat and drink. Jenny turned her own attention to her own injuries, quickly cleaning them with the antiseptic solution, spreading the antibiotic cream on some gauze and then dressing the worst of her cuts. When she'd finished she allowed herself to be directed to a well-worn sofa in the back room and then all she could do was wait.

★ ★ ★

'Jenny?'

Jenny stirred at the sound of her name, and for a moment had no idea where she was.

'Uh-huh . . . ' was the best she could come up with.

'Doctor Luc has asked me to take you to the clinic. So that he can check you out.' Armand said this with no trace of humour, so she figured he meant *look at your wounds*.

'I thought he was coming back here?' Her sleep-addled brain was not quite firing on all cylinders.

'He needs to stay with Salomen. He's in a bad way. He'll need to go to the mainland once we have a way to contact them.'

Jenny stretched, and instantly regretted it; the pain in her side was now sharp and demanding her attention.

Armand took in her expression.

'I think perhaps we should get you to Doctor Luc.' He held out his hand. Jenny ignored it with a roll of her eyes.

'I slipped and caught my side. It's just a bruise.' As she stood up, she felt the blood drain from her face. The pain was so intense now that she couldn't get any air into her lungs. She felt like she was frozen in time. The buzzing in her ears grew louder, and she didn't hear Armand call out to Francie for her help. Her knees buckled, and Armand caught her just before she hit the ground.

The next thing that Jenny was aware of was the sensation of being carried. It was a comfortable feeling for about half a second, the time it took for her to inhale. The pain then was so bad that she felt like she was being torn in two, and she couldn't keep a moan from her lips. She had looked after plenty of people with cracked ribs in her time, but had no idea that it was this painful. Her mind wandered a little as she decided that in the future she was going to be way more sympathetic.

'What happened?' There was a voice, and the sound of feet moving with a sense of urgency.

'She was asleep. When I woke her up, she told me that she had fallen; then, when she stood up, she fainted.'

Jenny knew that she recognised the voices, but still couldn't place them. There were brighter lights now, and a humming sound in the background.

'Lay her down over here,' the first voice said. 'Gently!'

Jenny felt herself laid on a raised bed; there was a pillow under her head. The light source moved with a creaking sound, and Jenny closed her eyes against the glare.

'You got the generator working?' Armand asked.

'Yes,' the other voice said in clipped tones. 'Was she complaining of pain anywhere in particular?' Jenny felt hands touching her head and moving logically down to the back of her neck.

'Her side, she said. Told me it was just a bruise.'

Jenny felt her torn shirt lift off of her skin, and even that small movement sent a wave of pain that was like an electric shock to her brain. She was awake. She opened her eyes and at the same time batted the hand away.

'Jenny, it's Luc. I need to check you for any injuries.'

'It's fine. Just a couple of bruised ribs.'

'So you're a doctor now too?' Luc said, but there was a glimmer of amusement in his voice.

Jenny went to shrug, and then sucked air through her teeth as the pain travelled from her side up into her head. She felt a hand on her shoulder.

'Would you please just relax and let me take charge, just this once?'

Jenny thought that was a bit rich, since they had only known each other for forty-eight hours, but she lay still as she felt cool hands gently press her abdomen.

'Any pain here?'

'No,' she said. The hands moved up and she watched Luc's expression. His eyebrows were raised.

'That's quite a bruise,' he said, and with the softest touch felt the ribs underneath. Jenny practically shot off the gurney she was lying on.

'Sorry.' And he sounded like he meant it. 'More than bruising, I'd say. More like a couple of broken ribs. We won't know until we can get the X-ray up and running. In the meantime, you need to rest. I'll ask Cynthia to get you some analgesia.'

Jenny nodded her thanks, and then remembered how she had injured herself. She reached out a hand for Luc's arm.

'How's Salomen?'

Luc's face was grave — an expression, Jenny thought, that didn't suit him.

'Fractured femur, evidence of internal bleeding. Spleen, I think, from the seatbelt. He's stable for now. It will be daylight in an hour. Hopefully, we'll be able to chopper him to the mainland. If not, I may be forced to operate here.'

Jenny took all this in and nodded. 'You have the facilities?'

'We have an operating theatre, but it's designed for minor ops, and we don't have intensive care facilities. Now, if you have no more questions, please can you follow my last instruction and rest? You aren't here to work, remember.' There was exasperation in his voice, but the trace of humour remained, and so Jenny relaxed back into her pillows.

Jenny listened to the bustling activity around her. It was all very familiar, but she was used to being on the other side of things. Her natural desire to help was continually raising its head; and so, even though she was exhausted, sleep would not come. Francie had brought Taavi to see his dad, and so Luc could give him a thorough check-over. Thankfully, it was clear that Jenny hadn't missed any more serious injuries on the boy. There was also a steady stream of locals with cuts and bruises, and one broken arm. Whilst it was busy in the clinic, it sounded as if the weather outside was starting to calm, which could only be good news for Salomen.

Jenny watched as Luc moved from patient to patient with calm efficiency. He was focused, clearly under some pressure, but always spent that little bit of extra time to reassure and comfort — something that not every doctor learned was important. Her mind drifted back to the sharp words in the car, when he had practically insisted that she couldn't stay in the hut. They had seemed so out of character, and coming from out of nowhere, that she just couldn't figure it out. Not that she needed to, she told herself firmly; the reason she was here was to work out what *she* wanted, not to try and solve the puzzle that was Luc — even if he had been kinder to her the two days she had known him than Kai had been in the three years they had been together.

The thought of Kai brought a storm of emotion, and she had to fight to maintain control. The urge to curl into a ball and cry was strong, but so was the pain in her side when she moved, along with the desire to start the grieving process in private. Another reason why she had travelled halfway round the world by herself.

'Do you need some more analgesia?'

Clearly Luc's careful attention had picked up the emotions on Jenny's face.

'No, I'm fine. Just have to remember not to move too much. How is Salomen?' she asked, keen to move the conversation on to a subject other than herself.

'He's holding on. The chopper should be here in thirty. We'll be heading out to the landing site shortly.'

Jenny watched as his eyes scanned the room, and she could see his dilemma. He had to leave with Salomen, but felt he was needed here too.

'I'm sure Cynthia can hold down the

fort, she seems very experienced.' She would have added that she could help out, but she suspected the response from him would not help his dilemma. His intensely protective nature towards her really was a puzzle.

Jenny thought she saw some of his tension ease a little. 'Cynthia has more experience than you and I put together,' he said with a smile. 'She has been here as long as I can remember.'

'Doctor Luc, are you saying I am old?' Cynthia said as she pushed a metal trolley with a dressing pack on it past Jenny's bed.

'More like a fine vintage of wine, Mama Cynthia. That only gets better with time.' He ducked his head a little as a sign of respect, and for a moment Jenny could see the young boy he was when he had lived on the island before. Cynthia made a *tsk* noise and batted him affectionately on the shoulder.

'The sooner you leave, Doctor Luc, the sooner you will be back,' Cynthia said as she busied herself dressing the wound of a young man who had arrived several minutes before.

'She's a mind-reader,' Luc whispered to Jenny in a semi-serious tone, before winking at her and then disappearing through a door to the room where Salomen was being cared for. Jenny listened as a vehicle pulled up outside, and then heard the unmistakable sound of a hospital trolley being pushed across the rough ground. Doors slammed, and then the wail of the ambulance siren started — loud at first, and then quieter as it drove away.

Jenny wasn't sure how much time had passed when the front door to the clinic burst open.

'Doctor Luc, Mama Cynthia. We need help!' The voice was urgent and anxious.

9

'How many?' Cynthia enquired urgently.

'The Havier house, collapsed in the storm. I have Josephine, Old Ben, and two of the kids, but the others are still trapped.'

Cynthia disappeared through the doors, and Jenny knew she couldn't just lie there any longer. With a wince, she rolled onto her side and slid her feet onto the floor. She stood up slowly, wanting to be sure to avoid a repeat of the fainting episode earlier, and took a few breaths. Once she was sure she wouldn't fall over, she made her way to the door.

'Jenny, where are you going?' Francie asked. 'You heard Doctor Luc — you need to rest.'

Jenny pushed the door open so that Francie could see what was happening outside, and the other woman protested no more, asking instead: 'What can I do?'

'Find some trolleys if you can, and make some room? Blankets, too, if we have any left.' And Jenny stepped outside.

Even though Jenny was used to seeing trauma close-up and personal, the scene was still a shock. In the back of a flatbed truck was an older man and a younger woman. They were covered in dust and blood, and it wasn't easy to immediately assess the level of their injuries. Cynthia had climbed into the back, and was in the process of trying to assess who was most badly injured and who needed help first. Her eyes flicked to Jenny, but she didn't order her back to bed as she had thought she would. Jenny could detect her carefully concealed concern, and the hidden message: *It's bad.*

'Nurse Jenny, we need a splint for young Enzo here. He has an open fracture to his humerus. Also a trolley, if we have one.'

Jenny nodded, and turned on her heel to get what she needed from inside the clinic. Once inside, she headed back through the door to the room that Salomen had been in, and found fully-stocked clinical shelves. She grabbed the supplies that she needed and headed back outside. The man who had driven the truck had lifted Enzo on to a trolley that Francie had brought outside. Jenny pulled on a pair of sterile gloves, and quickly poured saline solution over the wound. The boy moaned but lay still, a worrying sign. Jenny covered the open wound with a sterile dressing; and then, as carefully as possible, splinted Enzo's arm so that he would no longer be able to bend it. Once she was done, she nodded to Francie, and between them they wheeled him inside.

Jenny didn't need the electronic machine to tell her that Enzo's blood pressure was low and that he was in shock. She could tell from looking at him: despite his dark colouring, his lips were pale, and he was clammy and cold to the touch. Enzo needed fluids and pain relief, probably in that order. Jenny swiftly inserted a cannula into the back of the boy's hand. It was not easy, as he was starting to shut down, but Jenny had plenty of experience to guide her. Once she was sure the plastic insert was in the right place, she set up a bag of IV fluids, starting the process of rehydrating the boy and hopefully reducing his shock.

The door banged, and Cynthia appeared with the older man from the truck in a wheelchair. The man was breathing heavily and his eyes were glassy; he looked to be in a lot of pain. Cynthia and Jenny exchanged looks as Cynthia moved the wheelchair into the clinical room, which was clearly where the most poorly patients were treated.

'Enzo, I'm going to get you something for the pain,' Jenny said, resting a reassuring hand on the boy's forehead. 'Don't run off anywhere.' The boy managed a small smile, and Francie pulled up a seat and took hold of his hand.

'I'll be right back,' Jenny said before following Cynthia through the door.

'Complaining of central chest pain, radiating down his left arm. Uncle Jed was helping the others to dig out the rest of the family when the episode started. Has a history of angina,' Cynthia added, placing an oxygen mask on the face of the older man and pulling over the small ECG machine.

Jenny nodded. 'I'll get some pain relief for Enzo, and then come and give you a hand,' she said, knowing that right now Uncle Jed needed to feel that he was in familiar — and, more importantly, safe — hands. Cynthia nodded to a white cupboard attached to the wall.

'Fentanyl whistles in there. The red ones are for under-twelves. Have you used them before?'

Jenny shook her head. 'Not in Emergency, but I've seen them used out on the ambulances.' She unlocked the outer, and then inner, doors with the keys that Cynthia pulled from her pocket, found the red whistle, and went back to her patient.

'Francie, can you help Enzo with this? It has pain relief in; he needs to breathe it in and out slowly.'

Jenny unwrapped the whistle and mimed to the boy what he needed to do.

'Might make you feel a bit giggly, Enzo, but should help with the pain.'

'We'll be fine, Jenny. Go where you are needed.' Francie nodded her head in the direction of the treatment room, and Jenny nodded her thanks back.

Her worst fears were confirmed when she stepped back into the room. 'ST elevations,' was all that she needed to be told. Uncle Jed was having a heart attack. Laid on the trolley with its back propped up, he looked afraid and in pain.

'Here, Jed, take this,' Cynthia was telling him. 'I think your heart might not be too happy at you working so hard.'

'Aspirin?' Jenny asked.

Cynthia nodded. 'If I draw up some morphine, can you see if you can get a line in?'

'Yes.' Jenny quickly washed her hands before pulling on another set of sterile gloves. The veins on the back of Jed's hands were hard to feel, and so Jenny moved up his arm and into the crook of his elbow. Having applied a tourniquet, she gently tapped Jed's skin with the backs of her fingers and was rewarded for her efforts, finding a vein and quickly ensuring the needle was in the right place by the flashback of blood. She gave Jed a smile, and then stepped over to double-check the morphine dose with Cynthia.

'Do you have any GTN?' Jenny asked as Cynthia started to slow-inject the morphine, a small dose at a time. Cynthia pointed to another cupboard and Jenny found the spray. Gently lifting off the oxygen mask, she said, 'Uncle Jed, this should help with the pain. It can make your head feel a bit funny, but it will help your heart.'

Jed nodded. 'Take it all the time,' he managed to gasp out.

Jenny shook the small container and handed it over, watching whilst Jed self-administered the drug. She pulled up a stool and sat down, reaching out for Jed's hand, knowing that there was not much else they could do now until Luc returned. All they could do was wait.

It was probably only ten minutes or so, but to Jenny it felt like a lifetime. She had left the room briefly to check on the other patients; but the younger woman and the other boy, who turned out to be Enzo's mother and brother, had escaped with only a few cuts: Francie had seen to them. She returned to the treatment room praying that Luc would not be much longer. She almost felt as if Luc had read her mind, as the door swung open just as she was rechecking Jed's vital signs.

'What have I missed?' Luc said, pulling on a set of gloves.

It was several hours before all the patients had been treated. Luc had recalled the chopper, and both Uncle Jed and Enzo had been taken over to the mainland for further treatment. The other members of the family had been rescued and treated for minor injuries. Francie was making a much-needed cup of tea.

'Sit. All of you. You have been on the go for hours. You've looked after everyone who needs it. Now it's your turn to rest.' Francie indicated that they should go and find themselves somewhere to sit down. Cynthia led them to the covered veranda at the back of the clinic that looked onto a view of the mountains at the centre of the island. There was an odd selection of chairs here, plus a table, and Jenny sank gratefully into one of the free seats that had some old scatter cushions on it. She tried to move them quietly so that she could rest back comfortably, but she had not been as discreet as she thought she had.

'Do you need some more analgesia?' Luc asked, leaning forward from his own seat.

Jenny smiled. 'Not right now. Right now, I need a cup of tea more than anything.'

Cynthia smiled at her. 'If we are lucky, Francie may bring us some of her black cake. Just what you need after a day like this.'

As if on cue, Francie appeared with a tray laden with an old-fashioned, thin-spouted teapot, a mismatched set of teacups and saucers, and an old battered tin which promised cake. Once they had all been served, Francie asked the question that everybody wanted to know.

'Will Enzo and Uncle Jed be okay?'

Luc took a sip of tea.

'They were standing by to take him to the cath lab when we arrived; so, yes, I think so. Enzo is going to surgery later. He'll need some metalwork, no doubt, but he should be back to his usual self in a couple of months — and able to come home in a week or so.'

They all sat back in their chairs, drinking tea and eating cake.

'Is it always like this?' Jenny asked, then winced as she realised she had been musing out loud. 'I mean . . . ' She stopped. She wasn't really sure what she meant. The other three laughed.

'You mean, *Is it normally more laid-back?*' Francie asked

'Well, I was thinking the Caribbean would have a more relaxed pace of life, but so far it's not been that different from being at home.'

'That's because you seem to have confused work with this, which is supposed to be your holiday,' Luc said, and Jenny was instantly thankful that he hadn't said *honeymoon*. She didn't think she had the energy to try and explain that whole mess again.

'Even when I tell you to rest, I go away for half an hour and come back to find you saving people's lives.' His tone was teasing, and Jenny didn't take any offence.

'I couldn't just lie there and watch it happen,' Jenny said, 'any more than you could.' She turned and looked him in the eye; he raised an eyebrow, then shrugged his reluctant acknowledgement.

'You're both as bad as each other,' Francie said, in a tone that suggested that that was the end of it.

'Well,' Luc said, placing his empty teacup on the table, 'if you've finished, how about I escort you back home? You need to rest, and at least try and start your holiday.'

'I'll pop you round some supper later,' Francie said, and before Jenny could utter any comments along the lines of *Please don't put yourself out*, Francie waved her potential objections away. 'It's the least we can do for all the help you've given, and it's the St. Emilie way. We look after our own.'

Jenny could feel a glow inside her at the words. She had wanted to get away from everything at home; but she had to admit that, right now, having someone tell her she was basically family was what she needed to hear. She knew that it was probably just a combination of tiredness and what they had just had to deal with — not to mention, the pain in her side was getting more insistent.

'I'll bring you round some supplies too. I doubt Marcel has bothered to stock the place up for your arrival. Anything you need, you just ask, Nurse Jenny.'

Luc stood and held out a hand, which Jenny took gratefully. She wasn't looking for a repeat performance of earlier. There really was only so much fainting into a person's arms you could do before it became hard to look them in the eye. It wasn't as if she was a damsel in distress from a novel!

When she was standing, she realised that Luc was holding onto her hand when it was no longer strictly necessary. Now she was on her feet, she was fairly sure that she would be able to stay upright. His hand felt comforting and familiar in hers, and she was too tired to listen to the sensible part of her brain that was telling her she was on honeymoon without her husband, who had dumped her, and so probably shouldn't be holding hands with anyone. However, she allowed herself to be led back through the treatment room — where they stopped briefly so that Luc could gather up some medication for her in a plastic bag — and then out through the front door.

Luc opened the door to a car which had a green light on the roof and the words *St. Emilie Clinic* on the side, and watched her closely as she did her best to hide the pain of getting into her seat.

'Analgesia and bed as soon as we get back to yours,' he said, without a trace of embarrassment. Perhaps it was just Jenny's brain that went straight for a different interpretation of those words. She shook her head a little, as if to remind herself that she was not the most rational person at present when it came to aspects of the heart.

The journey took no more than a few minutes, but Jenny's mind seemed able to remember every step she had taken with Taavi the night before. She couldn't believe how much had happened to her since she left England. There was evidence of the storm everywhere: tree branches, rope, and fishing line were all across the road, as well as plastic bottles and cans.

'Going to take a while to clear up,' Jenny said, almost to herself.

'We're used to it. Last night was just a pretty typical storm for these parts.'

Jenny's mind travelled back to what had happened last night, and she shivered, which started a new wave of pain. She instinctively reached out an arm and cradled her side. She knew Luc had seen the gesture, but he didn't say anything.

'You mean you've had worse?' Jenny asked as Luc pulled the car up outside the hut.

'Well, we're just coming into hurricane season, so yes,' he said, walking round and opening the door for her. Jenny mentally rolled her eyes. Kai had said they would have an adventure; knowing him like she did, he probably thought that extreme weather conditions on your honeymoon ticked that particular box. She also suspected that the hurricane season was the reason he had booked the holiday for these dates: no doubt it had been cheaper that way.

'Doesn't matter what weather we have, the old shack always seems to remain standing. It has been here as long as I can remember, and seems to survive whatever St. Emilie throws at it.' Luc put a protective arm around her, and together they navigated a route through all the debris that had washed up from the beach.

'I'll ask Armand to send a couple of the boys up to clear this for you.'

'No need; I can do it myself.'

'You could, but you are supposed to be on holiday, remember?' Luc said as he opened the door to the hut.

Miraculously, everything inside was exactly as she had left it. The storm had not disturbed the hut at all. The sight of the bed with its covers thrown back could not have been more welcome. The pain in her side was insistent, and every breath, every slight movement, was like trying to eat with a toothache.

Luc led her over to the bed and helped her sit down, then walked to the fridge and pulled out a bottle of water. He took a strip of pills from the bag and popped two out in his hand, before handing first the pills and then the water to Jenny — standing watching as she swallowed, which nearly made her smile, since pain relief was about all she could think of at that moment.

Wincing as she laid herself back on the bed, she felt her legs being lifted up as Luc helped her. He pulled the covers over her. Then he drew his phone from his pocket and laid it on the bedside table.

'The clinic number is in there, and so

is Francie's. If I'm not at one, I'll be at the other. Call me if you need anything.'

Jenny nodded, feeling the weight of her eyelids tugging them closed.

'Anything at all,' Luc added — or had Jenny dreamt that? She was dimly aware of a hand on her forehead before the door was softly closed.

10

Jenny was running down the road. The rain seemed to be coming at her from all angles, so sharp and cold that it hurt her. She could hear a child calling her name. First it sounded like Taavi, and then like Tommy. Tommy's parents were running beside her, begging her to do something — but whatever she tried, she couldn't find him, couldn't help either of them. They were calling her name.

'Jenny? Jenny!'

A hand reached out for her and she tried to move away from it, knowing it was trying to stop her, to prevent her from getting to the boys. The movement pulled her up short as pain washed over her. She sat up with a gasp.

'You were having a nightmare,' the voice said, and as Jenny's eyes adjusted to the relative gloom, she saw that Luc was sat on the edge of the bed.

'I was trying to help Tommy — or Taavi?' She frowned as the splinters of memory made less and less sense the more seconds ticked by.

'Well, they are both fine — mainly thanks to your help,' Luc said, placing a calming hand on her arm.

'You know about Tommy . . . ' Jenny used her arms to sit herself up, and then took a breath to try and push away the pain.

'I had an email from Atlanta. He's responding well to treatment, and out of intensive care. He's out of danger.'

'His parents must be relieved.'

'Ecstatic, judging by the email they sent,' Luc said with a grin. 'It even has photos of him sat up in bed eating ice-cream. When you're up to it, you should drop into the clinic and I can show you.'

'I'd like that.'

Jenny was suddenly aware that Luc was sat close to her, and she wondered what on earth she must look like. She had fallen straight into bed when he had brought her back to the hut, so she must be covered in mud, with messy, rain-drenched-then-dried hair. She was sure it wasn't a good look. She reached a hand up to her head and tried to smooth it out, only succeeding in getting her fingers tangled in a knot of hair, twigs and leaves. There was no hiding it: she was a mess.

'Why don't you get cleaned up, and I'll get started on supper,' Luc said. He moved away into the kitchenette, and Jenny could see he had brought with him several bags: Francie must have been as good as her word.

'I thought Francie was coming,' Jenny said as she edged herself out of bed.

'I said I wanted to check on your injuries, and she seemed to think that was a good idea.'

Jenny couldn't help but smile. Luc had his back to her, so she wasn't certain whether he also suspected

Francie's motives for allowing Luc to come instead of her. She walked over to her suitcase, pulled out her washbag, some linen shorts and a floral light-cotton top, and headed for the shower room. It was only once she was inside with the door firmly shut that the sensible part of her brain started to kick in. What was she doing? She had picked out a new top which she knew showed off her figure, and her favourite shorts which showed off her long legs, the part of her which she always believed was her best feature.

Jenny stood paralysed for a moment. She couldn't very well go back out there and start going through her case again. What would Luc think? That she was a crazy woman who couldn't even decide what clothes to wear to an impromptu dinner between friends — not forgetting the fact that she was on her honeymoon, on her own! She stripped off the clothes she had worn to bed, and it was only then that she caught a glimpse of her side in the mirror. The bruising ran from her shoulder, down her side, and across what she could see of her back, in red and deep purple. For the first time since the injury had occurred, she indulged in feeling slightly sorry for herself. She had certainly done a number on herself when she fell!

She could hear the sounds of pans on the stove; not wanting to keep either Luc or her supper waiting, she turned on the water and stepped into the shower. It was surprisingly warm, considering that it came from a tank of water on the roof whose only heat source was the sun. Jenny washed her hair, and felt instantly better for it as she rinsed away the grime, blood, and goodness knew what else from her adventure the previous night. She tried to wrap her hair in a towel, but couldn't manage it one-handed — the pain in her side meant lifting her other arm that high not worth contemplating. She pulled on her clothes somehow, thankful that the design of the top meant she didn't have to try and figure out how on earth to get a bra on — let alone how much better her ribs felt without one! — and stepped back out into the main room.

The room was empty, and the door stood open. Jenny wondered briefly if Luc had been called back to the clinic for another emergency, but he reappeared through the door.

'Ah, there you are. Dinner is served on the terrace, madam,' he said with a mock bow.

'There's a terrace?' Jenny asked with a frown. If there was, she certainly hadn't noticed it before.

'No,' he said with a laugh, 'just a bit of beach that I put the table out on. It's lovely out there, but we can eat indoors if you think you will be too cold.'

'I'll be just fine,' she said, wishing she could stop him fussing over her wellbeing. She had come away to escape such endless sympathy, which was exhausting and only made her feel more guilty than she currently did.

'May I take your hand?' Luc enquired, holding out his with some flair.

'I think I can manage,' Jenny replied, but ensured she said it with a smile so as not to cause offence. For a moment, the cloud on Luc's face was back, but it seemed to pass quicker than it had before; once again, Jenny wondered if she had imagined it.

Luc stepped aside so that Jenny could walk through the door first, and she stopped so abruptly that he almost walked into her. Outside was the table from the kitchen, but with a clean, hand-embroidered tablecloth. There was a small vase with a flower, and two seats: one a stool, and the other a chair with cushions.

'The comfortable seat for the lady,' Luc said from behind her; Jenny realised she had been frozen to the spot, and moved.

'I would like to take credit, but Francie insisted that if I was going to come and sort out supper for you, I had to treat you like a lady.'

His smile was so relaxed that Jenny allowed herself to relax too. Perhaps it wasn't the romantic gesture she had instantly feared, but was instead Francie taking care of her. Jenny allowed herself to be directed to her seat, and sat herself down with care. She laughed when she saw a small plastic pot containing two white pills had been set out alongside a wine glass full of orange juice.

'No wine for you, I'm afraid,' he said, and she nodded and shrugged before closing her eyes briefly. 'How about you start with the pain relief, and I'll check the shrimp.'

Jenny swallowed down the pills and watched as Luc deftly turned the shrimp kebabs on the upturned oil tank that he was using as a makeshift barbeque.

'Hope you like seafood? Francie said she could tell by looking, but I wasn't so sure. She had a fresh delivery to the bar.'

'I love it, especially when it's barbequed in the Caribbean.'

'Well, in that case, you are in luck.' Luc picked up a plate and loaded it with shrimp that gave off a delicious spicy, smoky smell.

Jenny took a bite, and couldn't hold back her praise. 'That's amazing!' she declared before tucking in for another mouthful.

'Francie's secret recipe. I've no idea what's in it, but she made me up a pot.'

They didn't talk much as they ate — the food was too good — and it was a comfortable silence.

'So, what do you do when you aren't saving lives, Jenny?' Luc asked with the same twinkle in his eyes.

Jenny thought about that for a moment. In truth, the answer was *not much*, which brought her back round the same cycle of thoughts again — maybe that was why Kai had left her. Maybe that was why she would always be alone. She was all about work. She was boring.

She was aware that Luc was leaning back in his chair and studying her. 'I didn't think that would be such a difficult question to answer,' he said with a small smile.

'It's complicated,' she replied, returning his smile.

'Do I detect a link to your solo honeymoon?' He asked it in such a way that made her feel it was okay to tell him everything or nothing. He was not going to push her on it.

Jenny shrugged, and then winced. She really needed to remember not to do that. With one hand holding her side, she made up her mind. She had come to the island to get away from it all, to try and figure out what she was going to do next — but maybe an independent friend's advice would help that process. It wasn't as if Luc had ever met Kai, and so perhaps he could be honest with her — unlike her friends and family, who automatically defaulted to defending her. Which was sweet, but not what she needed right now. Luc took a swig of beer, and Jenny watched as his eyes scanned the beach.

'The sad story is that I was due to get married last week, and two days before, my fiancé decided that I was not the girl for him. I wasn't adventurous enough for him.'

Jenny took a sip from her bottle of water. Somehow, that wasn't as painful to say out loud as it had been at home. Maybe she was making progress after all. She felt in her heart that it couldn't be that simple, that there must be more to Kai's sudden decision — but even when pushed, that was the best he could come up with. He seemed oblivious to how wretched that made her feel. But then, anyone who dumped a girl two days before the wedding wasn't exactly blessed with a huge amount of compassion.

'Well, I have two things to say to that. Firstly, anyone who goes on holiday on their own to the other side of the world is adventurous in my book. Secondly, if you ask me, adventures are overrated.'

Jenny laughed now. 'Says the person who flew halfway round the world to be a doctor.'

Luc waved his beer bottle at her. 'That doesn't count, I'm afraid. I lived here for most of my childhood. This is not an adventure for me. This is home.'

It was a simple statement but Jenny couldn't help but feel that there was more weight to it than the words he had said.

'So, why did you decide to come home?' She said the words before she could chicken out. She felt brave having told him a truth that was so personal and painful to her.

'It just seemed like the right time. My contract with Abbeyfield had come to an end, and I needed a change. I guess it was always part of the plan once I had enough experience for the role.'

Jenny was sure that the shadow she had seen on other occasions was back again — fleeting, but definitely there. He clearly wasn't ready to tell her the whole story, and she knew how that felt, so she decided to let it go.

'Well, it's clear that everyone here was pleased to see you,' she said in what she hoped was an encouraging, changing-the-subject-slightly kind of way. Now she was rewarded with a smile, and it seemed genuine.

'It's home and family, really. Hard to explain, as it's so different from the UK.'

'It's wonderful,' Jenny said, and she meant it. 'I feel like part of a family, and I've only been here forty-eight hours. I was worried how it would be being here on my own, since I've never travelled so far solo, but it feels a little like home to me too — different, but home some-how.' She wondered if she was gabbling, the combination of tiredness and the pain relief kicking in.

'I think I'm waffling,' she said aloud, worried that she had sounded like she was claiming the island and its people as her own after such a short time, and that this might be offensive.

'You're in the Caribbean, Jenny,

that's how we talk about most things.' He smiled, and then she saw his doctor face appear. 'I think you need to get some more sleep.'

Jenny nodded, half-reluctantly. She didn't really want him to go. His company seemed easy and comfortable, without the crushing sympathy she had experienced recently from everyone else in her life, but she also could feel the pull of sleep.

'I think you're right,' she said, easing herself out of her chair. She took a few steps, and then it felt like the ground beneath her feet was moving. Her first thought was: *earthquake*. Surely they didn't have tropical storms *and* earthquakes here! The beach in the distance became blurry, and the trees seemed to be moving. She felt her feet leave the ground and wondered, somewhat distractedly, if she was falling . . . her mind drifted to how much that would hurt. She felt like she was floating, and it was only the drumming of Luc's heart in her ear that made her realise he had come to her aid once again. She felt safe in his arms as he gently carried her into the hut and laid her on the bed.

'Sleep. I'll leave you my phone again, and come back and check on you in the morning. If you need anything, anything at all, call me.'

It was more of an order than a request, and Jenny was reminded once again of Luc the doctor.

'I will, I promise. Thank you, Luc,' she said before she gave in to the tiredness. She wasn't aware of the tenderness that Luc showed as he pulled the covers across her to keep her warm, or the way he studied her sleeping face for a few moments before quietly leaving her to her dreams.

11

Jenny was up, and tucking into a selection of fruit that Francie had delivered via Luc, when she heard the Jeep pull up. She had opened all the doors and windows in the little hut to let in the light and fresh breeze coming off the ocean. Jenny stepped out through the open door and used her hand to shield her eyes from the sun as she tried to make out who was driving. It wasn't really hard to guess, since she knew so few people on the island.

'Morning. How are you feeling?' Luc asked, always a doctor first. He was dressed today in long board shorts and a white t-shirt. His hair seemed to have grown longer since they had first met, which Jenny knew was impossible, and its untidy, carefree style suited him perfectly.

'Much better, thanks. You didn't

need to come over and check on me. I would have called if I needed anything.'

'That was only one of my motives,' Luc said, stepping out of the Jeep. 'I've done my morning surgery, so I have a couple of hours free, and wondered if you fancied a tour of the island?'

He leaned back on the Jeep, giving off an air of casual interest. Jenny was sure that he was keen for her to go with him, but she was also certain that her 'guy radar' was faulty — after all, she had seen no sign that Kai was going to bail on her just days before their wedding. *He's probably just being kind*, she told herself firmly. She only half-believed it, but that was enough for her to agree to the trip.

'Sure. If you have time. Don't you need to get settled in?'

Luc laughed. 'Francie has done it all for me. No chance of me making important decisions like which drawer I want my socks in.'

Jenny raised her eyebrows.

'Relax, I was talking metaphorically. I

don't wear socks with flip-flops, I promise.' As if to prove it, he waggled a muscular tanned leg in her direction, which was wearing a worn flip-flop and definitely no sock.

They both laughed.

'Grab your sunnies and a hat. It's going to be a hot one.'

Jenny ducked back inside the hut and grabbed her floppy pink sunhat, sunglasses and suntan lotion. She paused briefly as she felt the urge to look for her phone, which was ridiculous since she had lost it at the site of the car crash two nights previously. Luc was waiting for her beside the Jeep, and took her hand and led her round to the passenger side.

'I'm not a complete invalid!' she protested.

'Just following Francie's orders, remember,' he said with a smile before slipping into the driver's seat.

'I have something for you,' he added, glancing at her briefly as he reversed the Jeep back out onto the road. 'In the

149

glove compartment.'

Curious, Jenny pulled at the glove compartment's door. Inside was a new mobile phone, wrapped in a bright pink bow.

'Thanks!' Jenny said, pulling off the bow. It was strange how naked she felt without her phone.

'Least I could do, since you lost it saving one of my patients. He's doing okay, by the way. They both are.'

'Glad to hear it.' Jenny switched on the phone and the screensaver appeared — a photo of Luc, looking particularly handsome and brooding, with a spectacular sunset as the background. Jenny stared at the image, not quite sure what to make of it. Was Luc trying to send her a very unsubtle message?

'Doesn't it work?' Luc asked, keeping his eyes fixed on the road. 'I asked Armand to pick one up for you. Maybe he didn't charge it.'

Jenny looked at Luc's frowning face, and was now fairly certain that the photo was Armand's mischief.

'It works fine,' Jenny said, trying hard not to grin. 'I'm just surprised at the screensaver you chose.'

Now Luc did take his eyes off the road for a moment: his face was all frown and innocence, so either he was a good actor, or as much a victim of the prank as she was. He took in her expression, and his confusion made her heart leap just a little. The next time he flashed a quick look at her, she held up the phone, and watched as his eyes widened before he remembered that he needed to look where he was going. With a slight swerve to correct his course, he slammed a hand against the steering wheel, accidentally catching the horn. The resulting sound made them both jump.

'I'm going to kill him,' Luc declared, before looking at her again. Jenny knew he was checking for her reaction, so she grinned back at him.

'He takes very model-like photos,' she said. 'Maybe he should consider a career change.' Then she could hold it in no longer, and the laughter burst from her, along with a slight wince at the pain it caused. Luc glanced at her once more, and then joined in.

'Okay, I won't kill him, but I have to get him back. That's the way things work here,' he added solemnly.

'I'm pretty sure that's the way things work everywhere when boys are involved!'

'Oh, please. Girls are some of the worst pranksters I know!' He was grinning now, and Jenny had to admit that she liked this side of him almost as much as she liked the focused, professional, doctor façade.

'You'll have to tell me about it sometime. I could probably use some inspiration in that area,' Jenny said, taking her eyes off of him to look out of the window. They were winding their way up a narrower road, heading inland. 'Where are we going?'

'One of my favourite places,' Luc said. 'You'll love it. It's one of the best-kept secrets of the island. Only we islanders know about it, and we never tell off-landers about it.'

Jenny raised an eyebrow. 'Aren't I an off-lander?' She really wanted him to say *no*, which told her that she needed to get a grip on herself. She was here to figure out what she wanted from life, not immediately fall in love with another man. She couldn't help but admit to herself that it was flattering to have another man's attention — particularly since she had been dropped in such a public and humiliating fashion — but, however good it felt, it wasn't what she needed. It wasn't fair on Luc, either. If he did like her then she needed to make it clear that she was not in a good place and if he didn't, well then she needed to save herself the embarrassment of another romantic *faux pas*.

'Jenny, you should know by now that you have been officially adopted — ' She smiled. ' — and there's nothing you can do about it, I'm afraid,' he finished in mock-seriousness.

'I think I could get used to it.'

Soon they were off the tarmacked road and heading across country on dirt tracks through dense forest. It felt at times like the trees were pressing in on them, and the air entering through the rolled-down windows was heavy and close. Jenny didn't think she had ever seen such vibrant colours, so many greens and flowers. It was a noisy world, too, with calling birds and a constant background hum of insects.

'This is amazing,' Jenny said softly, as if she didn't want to disturb the wildlife around her.

'You haven't seen anything yet,' Luc said, pulling the Jeep over into a small clearing. 'Now we need to walk — only about ten minutes or so, and it's fairly flat. Are you up to it?'

'Are you kidding? I'm on holiday,' Jenny said, and was out of the Jeep before she finished saying the words.

He held out a hand to her and she took it, her hand fitting neatly into his.

Luc led her into the forest on a path that Jenny would have missed entirely, but Luc seemed certain where it started and where it led. Once on the path, it was clear that it was used, but Jenny suspected its regular visitors were animals rather than people. She couldn't help but glance nervously at the dense surroundings, trying to remember what she had read about the wildlife on the island.

'Relax, Jenny, it's perfectly safe.'

Something brushed against her free hand, and she let out a shrill squeal before she could stop herself. Luc turned, but instead of showing concern he simply grinned at her.

'There's nothing out there that will hurt you — remember, everything is more scared of you than you are of it.'

Jenny was less than convinced. She had seen enough people recently returned from exotic holidays with weird ailments — some the result of encountering native creatures — to know that was probably not true.

'Yeah, you do know that St. Jude's has a tropical diseases unit, don't you?' She felt herself grip his hand more tightly at the thought of what might be out there waiting to bite, sting, or sink its fangs into her bare ankles.

'You forget I was raised here. I know what to look out for. I'll keep you safe.' He turned now, and his earnest expression nearly made Jenny forget her concerns — but only nearly. It was hard to relax and enjoy the spectacular surroundings when you were afraid of the nasty surprises they surely hid.

All of these thoughts, though, were lost to her when Luc led her into a clearing. The sound of rushing water drowned out all other noises, and Jenny found herself standing beside a clear pool, with a waterfall spilling down the cliff at the far end of the clearing. Luc had been right: it was truly beautiful — in fact, it had all the hallmarks of paradise.

Luc led her to an outcrop of rock that formed a natural diving board into the cool waters. He sat down, removed his flip-flops, and dangled his feet in the water below. Jenny followed suit. The water was surprisingly cold, but the movement from the waterfall meant that she felt as if she was using a very fancy foot-spa.

'Well, what do you think?' Luc said, leaning back on his arms so that he could take in the view of the trees overhead, which seemed to be reaching out for each other, forming a natural canopy to the outdoor pool.

'It's breathtaking,' she answered.

'You wait; when your ribs have healed, we'll come back and swim.' He turned to look at her and she met his gaze. 'The local kids come here after school, and it gets pretty rowdy then; but in the daytime during the week, it is our island's most secluded piece of paradise.'

He seemed to frown a little then, as if he'd said too much or meant something entirely different. Jenny hated to see the turmoil; and, as always, didn't like to see anyone squirm.

'I'd love to,' she said in a firm, *just-as-friends* kind of way. 'Did you come here much when you were a kid?'

She watched as his eyes seemed to drift away to another time. 'We all did. Fraser and I used to sneak out of school early so that we'd get the best spot to jump from the top.'

Jenny followed his eyes right up to the top of the waterfall. Her own eyes widened: it had to be over fifty feet high.

'You jumped? From up there?'

Luc shrugged, but the dreamy look had been replaced by something else.

'When you're a kid, you think you're invincible. It's only later in life that you learn that's not the case.'

'Where's Fraser now?' She tilted her head to one side, studying him closely. 'Doesn't sound like a French name.'

Luc sat forward so suddenly that Jenny was sure he was going to launch himself into the water.

'Scottish,' he said, resting his elbows

on his knees. Jenny sat forward too, and reached out a tentative hand for his arm.

'Scottish . . . like your dad?' she asked, so softly she wondered if Luc could hear her over the rush of the waterfall.

'Dad picked the name for their first son, and Mum for their second.'

Jenny nodded, wondering if she was starting to understand the secret that Luc was keeping.

'Fraser, your brother.' She said it more as a statement than a question. 'You don't have to talk about him if you don't want to.' She wanted him to tell her, of course; she knew that she cared about Luc — probably more than she should, given her own romantic circumstances — but she also knew how hard it was with everyone trying to press you into describing how you felt in the face of an event that had caused you indescribable pain. She was sure that she and Luc shared that pain, even if their circumstances were different.

Many moments passed and Jenny wondered if he was angry with her for asking — no, pressing — him to tell her. His back and shoulders were stiffly turned away from her, and his knuckles were clenched so tightly on the rock edge that the whiteness shone through the tan.

'I'm sorry. I shouldn't have pressed you,' Jenny said, voicing her concerns out loud.

She studied his still form, not knowing what to do next. She felt as if she had destroyed something precious, although they barely even knew each other. The pain seemed sharper than she would have expected.

'You didn't. I brought it up,' Luc said, but with his face turned away from her she couldn't read his emotions.

Jenny turned her attention back to the water swirling around her feet. Whatever internal battle Luc was fighting, it was a mirror of her own all the times she had been faced with people asking how she was after Kai left. To experience that in public, even with well-meaning people, only added to the battle: the desire to keep what you felt private fighting with the desire to receive some comfort from those that cared. Without conscious thought, she moved her hand closer to him, and gently linked her little finger over his. She expected him to pull away, but he didn't.

A beep sounded, and the noise was so alien that it made Jenny jump more than if she had heard the roar of a loud and hungry wild animal.

Luc pulled something from the waistband of his shorts and read the typed words on what turned out to be an old-fashioned pager, something Jenny hadn't seen in use for years.

'We have to go,' Luc said, and when he turned to her she could see the full agony in his face. She wanted to reach out and try and wipe some of the sadness off it. 'I'm sorry, it's an emergency.' He got to his feet, and she scrambled to hers. As if remembering at the last minute that she was still not completely healed, he reached out for her arm to steady her.

'I shouldn't have brought you here,' he said as he led the way quickly down the path. 'I haven't been back since . . . ' His voice tailed off, and Jenny reached out for his hand. He stopped so abruptly that she nearly walked straight into him. The look of anger on his face made her recoil in shock.

12

It was like the shadow she had seen before, but multiplied by a thousand. Jenny opened her mouth to speak, but no words came out, and in truth she had no idea of what to say. She had no notion of what she could have done that would cause such a reaction. It was clear that the memories of Luc's brother were painful, that something terrible had happened to him, but it didn't explain what she felt — that she had personally hurt him.

Jenny stood stock-still, her limbs seemingly unable to obey her, and watched as Luc turned away from her and started to stride down the path. She had to jog to keep up, her fear pushing away the pain of breathing in sharp, quick breaths that seemed to batter her broken ribs. The look on his face made her afraid that he would leave her behind if she didn't keep up.

They made it back to where Luc had parked the Jeep in less than five minutes. When Jenny arrived, breathless with effort and fear, he was standing leaning on the vehicle with his back to her. She took a moment to try and calm herself. Her fear had been replaced by anger. Even if she had upset him, there was no need for him to react to her in the way he had. She was acutely aware of the sensible part of her brain that had warned her of making a new attachment to anyone in her current delicate state. She tried to smooth the anger from her face, knowing that any response she made now might release all the stored-up pain from her break up with Kai.

She walked to the other side of the Jeep, pulled open the door, and eased herself in. She fastened her seatbelt, and when she heard the other door open she turned her face to look out of the window, as if there was something deeply fascinating there keeping her attention. She could feel Luc's eyes on her, but she wasn't ready to speak, even if she could find the words.

She heard a stifled sigh that was not without both anger and regret, but still couldn't bring herself to respond. That was what Kai had always done: no matter the circumstances, no matter who was in the wrong, it had always been up to her to make the first move.

They drove in silence, and to Jenny it was as if the surroundings had lost some of their beauty. She made herself focus on all the things she had planned to do whilst she was away from everything at home. She had books to read and a life to plan. That was what she should be thinking about. She had no room in her mind for the games that men in her life always seemed to end up playing. The silence, which had been comfortable before, now seemed the awkward distance of strangers who didn't know what to say to each other. Jenny told herself firmly that it was true: they *were* strangers. Thrown together in difficult circumstances, true — but, in reality, she knew nothing about Luc, and he knew nothing about her. Those circumstances had created an illusion of closeness which had just been shattered by what, Jenny wasn't sure.

One thing she did know was that she didn't have room in her life for more emotional baggage. She had so much to process, and adding more would only cause her more pain. She needed to let it go. She needed Luc to let go of the illusion too, and that would never happen if she continued to show the hurt he had caused her.

'If you need to head straight back to the clinic, I can walk home.' She did her best to keep her voice even, and to hide the turmoil of emotion she was struggling to keep at bay.

'You need to rest. I can drop you back on the way.' Luc kept his eyes fixed on the road, and the only sign he was feeling anything was the way he was gripping the steering wheel. Jenny wondered if he was now feeling guilty, for the way he had reacted and for the way he had made her run after him. She pushed the thoughts aside and tried to focus on which book she was going to read. The effort was pointless, sat so near to Luc, who radiated anger and upset and was too difficult to ignore. She wondered if she should try and bridge the gap between them again to try and smooth over the feelings between them.

'I'm fine, really. The fresh air will do me good, and I plan to read all afternoon.'

He turned his head so quickly that she almost jumped in her seat.

'No, you're not, Jenny. You are two days post-rib fractures, and I just dragged you up half a mountain.' His anger had caused her pain, and she was sure now that he knew it, and that the anger he had displayed was now turned firmly inward.

'Nonsense,' she said firmly in a tone she frequently used as a nurse, one that brooked no disagreement. 'You know as well as I do that the last thing you should do after any minor accident is lie around in bed all day. I don't need to tell you the risks associated with that.'

She studied him closely to see how he would react, but his face gave nothing away except fierce concentration, and she knew that was just a shield. It was clear from the way he had driven them to their destination that he probably could have done so with his eyes shut. But he said nothing, and when they reached a fork in the road that was vaguely familiar, Jenny knew that he had ignored her and was going to drive her home despite her protests.

When he pulled up the Jeep in front of the little shack that had quickly become her home, he looked as if he wanted to say something. Jenny waited a few moments to see if he would, sure that if they could clear the air she would be able to forget about what had just happened and focus on all the other things in her life . . . but the silence stretched out and she just felt the unease return.

'Thank you for taking me to the waterfall.' She opened the car door and stepped outside. 'Seeing that part of the island makes me feel like I'm truly on holiday.' The words seemed formal and stiff, but perhaps that was how she should speak to someone she barely knew. She felt his eyes seek out hers, and she couldn't look away. So brown and deep, and holding everything which he didn't seem to be able to say out loud.

Jenny was the first to react, her sensible side reminding her that he had an emergency to attend to, and didn't have the time to sit around and try to make sense of what had just happened between them.

She closed the door. 'You'd better go. Your patients need you.'

Those words seemed to spur him into action, and with one last look at her he put the Jeep in gear and drove away. Jenny allowed herself to stand and watch him go. How could she feel so much for someone she had just met? She wished her friends were here so she could ask them. She felt her new phone in her pocket, and wondered about texting them. The thought almost made her laugh out loud. She could almost hear Steph's response. Steph was a firm believer that Jenny needed to get back out there, and would no doubt advise that a rebound fling was just what she needed to move on from Kai. But Jenny knew that the emotions she felt for Kai ran too deep to just be pushed aside like that.

As she opened her front door, she knew that was not the only reason. Luc radiated pain as she did, and there was no way she wanted to add to that burden, either for him or for herself.

Jenny ran her finger along the row of books she had lined up on one of the shelves. She moved quickly past a couple which were clearly self-help books that Steph had given her just before she left. She wasn't sure she was ready for all that life-affirming, empowering talk just yet. There was a book on Mary Queen of Scots, one that she had selected as being 'good for her', but that didn't appeal either. At the end of the row were various chick-lit novels, and she picked one at random. She had found in a cupboard a rolled-up canvas hammock; and, outside, two trees that had ties, which told her that was where it was supposed to be suspended. She picked up her book, sunglasses and bottle of water, and went outside. Getting into a hammock was not easy at the best of times, and she could feel her ribs protesting despite the pain relief she had taken; but once she was lying down, she knew she had found it. She was in her own personal paradise.

The buzzing in her pocket woke her. For a few moments she wondered if she was on a ship, as she felt sure she was gently rocking. She opened her eyes and remembered the hammock, the island . . . and an image of Luc's angry face also came unbidden. She pushed it away as she wriggled so that she could pull her phone from her shorts. The flashing light told her she had a received a text message. Since she had only texted her mum to reassure her that all was well but she had lost her phone, without going into any of the dramatic circumstances of her injury, there were two choices as to who it could be: her mum or Luc. She sighed and rearranged herself in to a more comfortable position. The phone buzzed again with another message, and so she was sure now it was her mum — who she adored, and who was probably one of the most impatient people she had ever met when it came to technology. She always expected an instant reply.

Pressing the button to turn on the phone, Jenny was rewarded with the brooding photograph of Luc that Armand had set as her Screensaver. She frowned, thinking that she should take a photo of the beach — or somewhere else equally beautiful — to replace it. She felt certain that seeing Luc's image every time she used her phone would not help her create the distance between them that she felt they both needed. She pressed her finger to the message icon, and the number that appeared made her freeze. It was one she never had to look up, since she had memorised it after their first date. The message was from Kai.

13

Jenny stared at her phone. If Kai had contacted her on her old phone, then a photo of them together would have appeared on the screen. She would have known it was him even before that, since she had set up a separate ringtone and text alert just for him: something he'd seemed to find highly amusing, and which now even the thought of made her cringe. Perhaps Kai's reaction hadn't been the teasing that lovers shared, but in fact mocking how hard she had fallen for him when, it seemed to her now, that he could have cared very little for her — if at all.

Since it wasn't her phone, the only person who could have given Kai her number was her mum. Which seemed unlikely as her mum, normally a placid person, had threatened all sorts of personal injury on Kai when she had found out what he had done to her only daughter. Her mum would never give him her number unless it was something of grave importance, something really bad.

Her hand was shaking now as her mind reeled at all the possibilities, all the things that could have gone wrong in the past few days. One of the reasons that she was hurting so badly was that, whatever he had done, she still loved him. The fear seemed to galvanise her into action, and her thumb found the 'read' button before she could procrastinate anymore.

Hi Jenny. It's Kai. Jenny blinked; as if he could even think that she wouldn't recognise his number! She felt with a gut wrenching certainty that he probably couldn't recall hers, even if his life depended upon it. *Your mum says that a bill for the wedding has arrived at the flat. Can you sort it? You said you were happy to pay everything. Ta*

Jenny's eyes widened, and she sat up with such angry force that she tilted the balance of the hammock and found herself unceremoniously flung to the floor. The anger masked any pain or embarrassment. In fact, she was so incandescent that her mind raced with furious retorts.

'Are you alright?' a familiar voice shouted as she heard the sound of feet running across the sandy earth. Jenny groaned — not just with the reminder her bruised body was giving her that somersaults out of hammocks were not something she should be doing right now, but with that deep-seated, cheek-burning embarrassment that comes when you are making a fool of yourself and someone has seen you. And not just anyone, but Luc. She twisted her head as she tried to untangle herself from the canvas-and-rope mess that she found herself in.

'Hold still,' the voice commanded. 'You're making it worse.'

She felt hands grip her legs, and the tight pull of the ropes lessen. The canvas was unwrapped, and two strong arms lifted her from the remains of her once-comfy hanging seat. She felt herself gently turned to an upright position.

'Have you hurt yourself?' Jenny looked up into Luc's face, and for a moment saw a flash of amusement, a sign that perhaps the old Luc had returned. Jenny shook her head and watched as he pulled a leaf from her tangled hair.

'Only my pride — as usual,' she added, and for this she was rewarded with a grin. 'How is it that you always turn up at my most mortifying moments?' she asked as she pulled her clothes into line and started to try and brush off some of the sand.

'Just lucky, I guess?' And he laughed.

He'd laughed. Jenny couldn't quite believe the transformation. She almost felt as if she had dreamt the whole situation where he had seemed so angry and distant from her. In front of her was the Luc from the plane and the dinner. She frowned at the confusion she felt — it was like he was Jekyll and Hyde. A hand reached for her, and this time the voice held concern.

'Are you sure you're not injured?'

Jenny looked up and smiled, pushing aside the confusing thoughts. 'Really, I'm fine. Would you like a drink?' she said, deciding that changing the subject was probably the way to go.

'Why don't you sit down?' he said, indicating the chairs by the small table they had dined at only the night before. 'I'll make the tea, and you can tell me how you managed to fall out of your hammock.'

Jenny sat and watched him walking into the shack, his shoulders gently shaking as he laughed — no doubt at the image of her being catapulted out of her hammock. The time it took Luc to make the tea gave Jenny a few moments to think. She had to decide if she was going to tell Luc the full story or not. Would it embarrass her further, or would it help to have someone else disclaim Kai's appalling behaviour? Or would Luc think her more the fool for thinking she could marry a person who could treat her in such a cavalier manner?

The chink of china being set before her brought her back to the here and now.

'Are you hungry? I found some leftover black cake.'

Jenny nodded, thinking that eating would delay the inevitable for a few moments. Her stomach rumbled, giving her away.

'Sounds like you forgot about lunch?' Luc said, raising one eyebrow in mock disapproval.

'More like I fell asleep,' she said without thinking, and then worried that even a vague reference to the events of that morning would break the spell that Luc seemed to be under.

'All that exercise,' he said mildly before sipping at his tea.

Jenny blinked in surprise, his comment again making her wonder if she had imagined the whole thing.

'Sorry that I had to rush off,' he added, but seemed unable to look at her.

'That's okay. I'm a nurse, remember? I get it,' she answered, thinking that this was probably safe ground. One thing was for sure: she would be considering this conversation carefully later, when she was alone, to try and figure out just what was going on. Luc seemed to feel she had accepted his apology — which, she guessed, she kind of had — and continued, rubbing his hands together.

'So tell me, how exactly did you manage to fall out of your hammock?'

Jenny rolled her eyes and let out an exaggerated sigh.

'I got a text.'

'And does that phenomenon normally make you fall over?' he asked, and Jenny could see the grin tugging at his lips again.

'Not usually; only when it's from the man who dumped me two days before our wedding to ask me to pay one of the wedding bills.'

Luc choked, but managed to turn away from her so that his tea sprayed over the ground rather than the table.

'I'm sorry — he did what?'

There was the angry indignation that Jenny felt she was owed considering the circumstances. The fact that it came from Luc was slightly troubling, but since he was basically the only person on the island who knew about her situation, he would have to do, however complicated that might make matters.

'How did he even get your number?'

'He says my mum gave it to him.'

Luc raised an eyebrow. Jenny sighed; now she had had a bit more time to think about that, it was about as likely as her mum shaving off all her hair.

'I suspect my mum gave my number to some of my friends, and one of them gave it to him.' She frowned again; she couldn't imagine who would do that. 'They probably posted on social media or something.' She might have to check that out, although she knew that she didn't want to read anything on there about her failed wedding.

'Wow. That's cold,' Luc said. 'I'm sorry.'

And there it was. Sympathy, the thing she had been trying to avoid as much as she could, the reason why she had travelled halfway round the world by herself.

'Don't be. It's just more evidence that I made a lucky escape. It would have been worse to find out who he was after we were married.' She said the words calmly, but knew that she was really trying to convince herself. Another wave of pain hit her, and it was so swift and sharp that she felt like she couldn't breathe. How could Kai do this to her? How could he be so callous? He was right, of course: she had said she would pay for the wedding. After all, she was good with money and he was awful, but she didn't mind — or, at least, she hadn't at the time. Perhaps that was why he had considered marrying her. Perhaps he thought that she would keep him financially afloat so that he could continue to go off on his reckless adventures like a teenager.

This thought brought another wave of pain, and to her shock she found that she was sobbing. She had made no conscious decision to cry, to be upset, but it just seemed to burst from her.

Without knowing how it happened, she found herself once again in Luc's arms. He lifted her from her seat and then sat down with her, cradling her to his chest. He said nothing, which Jenny was grateful for; just held her tight, and gently stroked her hair. Jenny knew that the emotion had come so unbidden that it was not going to be stopped, so she let it out. All of it: for the first time since it had all happened, she let herself express the pain she felt. It made her body shake with grief, and her sobs turned to silent wails, but all the while Luc held her tightly, not saying a word.

Jenny wasn't sure how much time had passed. She felt she had been in Luc's arms forever, and had no desire to leave, except for a nagging thought that she could not pin down.

'Don't you have patients to see?' she asked suddenly as her mind grasped what had been out of reach. He had dealt with the emergency, but surely he had others who needed his attention.

'I'm on my rounds as we speak,' he said softly, and his voice was muffled by her hair as he rested his head gently on top of hers. Jenny allowed herself a smile.

'And do you always give your patients such hands-on care?' she asked, knowing that she shouldn't but not able to help herself.

'Only one.'

Jenny felt her heart leap, and the words seemed to allow her to put distance between the torrent of emotion and where she found herself. She knew she should move, should gently disentangle herself from Luc's arms. She knew now for certain that Luc could never be a rebound affair. He was already more important than that to her, and she couldn't do that to him. She had so much pain and distrust to work through, there was no way she was in a position to risk her heart again — however reckless she might feel at that moment.

As if he could sense her thoughts, Luc's embrace loosened, and she took the opportunity to find her feet and stand up.

'I'm sorry you had to see that,' she said, not knowing what else to say.

'Don't be,' Luc said, and those simple words made her heart skip a beat. Why was he so understanding? It was certainly not helping her resolve. She forced herself to pull up an image of his angry face from earlier, to remember how she had felt on the drive back, but those images and feelings felt a million miles in the past and she couldn't capture them enough to prevent her from doing what she did next. Luc's eyes had not left hers, and she could feel herself being pulled back to him. She took a step, and was standing so close to him that she could feel his breath on her face. He lifted a hand to cradle her cheek, and his eyes told her all she needed to know. She leaned down and kissed him, gently brushing her lips against his. She studied him, needing to be sure that she wasn't misreading any signals — but his eyes flashed with desire, and she knew she had been right.

She felt his hand at her back, drawing her body closer to his, and this time he kissed her. The flash of heat that ran through her was like nothing she had ever felt before, and she ran her hands through his hair as she felt their tongues meet. After what felt like days, they broke apart, both needing to take a breath. Jenny leaned away, but Luc's arms held her tight. Every part of her hummed with the sensation of being close to him, and was calling out for more. Jenny's brain struggled to remember all the reasons why she shouldn't, but she could come up with none that made her want to step further away.

Luc's eyes watched her carefully, and once again she felt as if he could read her mind. He pulled her gently on to his lap, arms encircling her, and she nestled her head under his chin.

'I hope I didn't overstep,' he said softly.

Jenny laughed in return. 'I think I was the one who started the stepping!' She could feel Luc's rumble of mirth through his chest.

'I should warn you, I've always had terrible timing.'

'I should warn you . . . ' Jenny had been going to say something funny and light in return. But she knew deep down, like a burning coal in her stomach, that she should be warning him against falling for her. She was damaged goods. She knew she couldn't trust her own feelings in anything right now. She would not, could not, risk hurting him.

'I know,' was all that Luc said.

'I'm sorry. I'm all over the place. I've

no idea what I want or how I feel.'

'I know that too.'

She shifted on his lap so that she was facing him. She lifted a hand to his face to ensure she had his full attention.

'I don't want to hurt you.' There, she had said it out loud. She had warned him.

'You won't.'

'You can't know that. I can't know that.'

'But I know you.'

Jenny felt herself stiffen at the words.

'No, you don't.' The words had come out with anger — not at Luc, but at herself. She knew she shouldn't be doing this and probably wouldn't have if he had not turned up at the moment he had. Luc was right: he had terrible timing.

'Jenny. I'm not asking you for anything. You've told me enough about your recent past for me to know that that would be unfair. I'm not asking you to protect me from anything, including your jumbled-up feelings. But

188

this — ' And he tightened his grip and kissed her cheek lightly, all the while watching for her reaction. ' — this feels right to me.'

Jenny nodded. Whatever her doubts and reservations, it felt right to her too.

'But I care about you,' she said

Luc chuckled. 'Well, that's fortunate, or this could have been very awkward.'

'You know what I mean,' she said, feeling cross that he wasn't listening to what she was really saying.

'I do, and that is what I am trying to tell you. You are not responsible for me or my feelings. You have been honest with me about where you are at; and I want to be with you, knowing all of that. You have nothing to be afraid of. I'm a grown man, and if I want to risk getting hurt, then that is my choice.'

He stopped and let her mull over his words.

'Love is a risk, Jenny, whoever and whenever you find it with. But, unless you are prepared to take that risk, you will never truly find it.'

14

They sat together until the sun set. As the shadows grew longer, the temperature dropped suddenly, and Jenny shivered. Without warning she was lifted in Luc's arms and carried back into the shack.

'It's getting cooler; you might want to grab a sweater,' Luc said.

Jenny, still a little dazed from her impromptu mode of transport, just stared at him. They had sat in silence for hours but she had yet to give him any kind of answer. Luc, for his part, seemed content, as if he knew that she could not be rushed into making a decision after such a difficult day.

'Francie has asked us to a family dinner. That's what I came out to tell you.'

Jenny's eyes widened in surprise — not at the invitation, but at the casual tone of Luc's words. She opened her mouth to speak, but he moved across to her and put a finger to her lips.

'We talked, and now you need to think. I understand, Jenny. Go and get changed for dinner with the family. No strings attached, I promise.'

Jenny stood still, not quite believing what had happened in such a short time, Luc's understanding was so unexpected, and so unlike Kai, that she felt the tears gather behind her eyes once more.

'It's okay, Jenny, really,' Luc said with a smile, before giving her a gentle push in the direction of the tiny bathroom. 'I'll wait out in the Jeep; take your time.'

Ten minutes later and Jenny was ready. She had changed into long linen trousers, a cotton top, and — in deference to the slightly cooler weather — grabbed her one and only cardigan. It wasn't as if packing warm clothes should be top of the list when you were going on holiday to the Caribbean.

She let her mind wander across all the events of the day. Even Kai's text seemed to have lost some of the power it had over her. Of course, her practical mind was wondering what the bill was for and how much it would cost her — for a wedding that had never happened! — but even that seemed distant, as if it was someone else telling her about their own situation rather than it being about her life.

She reached a hand for the door and told her mind firmly to stop. There was no way she could figure all this out, not in the time it would take her to walk to the Jeep. She needed to push it away and focus on what was right in front of her.

There was one problem with that, she thought, as she opened the door and saw Luc leaning back in the driver's seat with his legs resting through the open window: a major part of her confusion was sat in front of her, and she was going to have dinner with him.

At that moment, Luc seemed to realise that she was there and turned to look at her, his smile broad and encouraging. Luc, at least, seemed to have no qualms about what they had talked about. He pulled his legs back into the Jeep and reached across to open the door. Jenny knew this was her cue, and so tried to focus once again on the fact that it was a family dinner and got in beside him.

They sped down the road to the little town and Luc pulled up outside Francie's bar. He jumped out and walked around to Jenny's side, opening the door and offering her his hand. He grinned at her, and she got the feeling that his gentlemanly actions were not just for her benefit. She was right. Francie appeared at the door and nodded at him in approval before stepping towards Jenny and pulling her into a tight hug.

'Good to see Doctor Luc is taking good care of you, Jenny,' Francie said, her accent strong and deep.

Jenny smiled back. 'Thanks for the invitation.'

'Tsh. You are always invited, Nurse Jenny. I was beginning to wonder if you would ever come, which is why I sent Luc to fetch you.' She smiled warmly, and Jenny felt once again as if she were part of the family.

'Come, come. The food is ready. What took you so long?' Francie said, turning her gaze to Luc, who simply shrugged as if there were no explanation worth the telling. Jenny felt herself blush a little as she remembered exactly why they were late. Luc moved to her side, pulled her hand into his, and gave it a light squeeze. He raised an eyebrow and smiled, which Jenny took to mean that her hammock acrobatics would not be used as polite dinner conversation. She squeezed his hand back gratefully. Although she was used to those kinds of embarrassing disasters, she did not enjoy reliving them, and doing so would no doubt give rise to the question as to why she had fallen out of the hammock

— that was definitely something she wanted to avoid mentioning, at all costs.

They moved through the main body of the bar, which was bustling with patrons, and out to the back yard, which was quieter. Luc directed Jenny to a seat at the table. Armand was already there, as was Francie's daughter Jocelyn, and Cynthia, as well as a few other faces that Jenny didn't recognise. The introductions were brief and loud, and Jenny was sure she would not remember who everyone was, or how they were related for that matter. Luc sat next to her and offered her a bottle of beer which he opened with the palm of his hand, a trick that Jenny had never managed to master. Once his own was opened, he offered up his bottle and she lifted hers to his in a toast.

When Jenny had eaten more than she thought humanly possible, she became aware of a heated conversation at the end of the table between Armand and a man named Pascal, supposedly a distant cousin.

'I'm telling you, man, it will hit us hard.'

Armand waved a hand as if to ward off a fly.

'Don't talk such nonsense. All those experts say it will miss us. Might get a bit of the wind's tail-end, but that will be that.'

Jenny turned to Luc, who was listening in with mild interest.

'What will hit us hard?'

Luc smiled, and leaned towards her so that only she could hear.

'Pascal is a storm chaser. Nothing he likes more than to be the bearer of bad-weather news. Armand says it's because Pascal has English in his blood from way back.'

'There's going to be another storm?'

Luc choked out a laugh.

'Of course, it's the season, but that's not what Pascal is talking about.'

Jenny took a sip of beer, as she tried to remember just how many she had drunk and raised a questioning eyebrow.

'Pascal is talking about the legend which says we will one day get hit with a storm such as never seen in this century or the last.' Luc spoke in a low, deep voice that made him sound like a very solemn news presenter. Jenny giggled.

'Like the big earthquake that is going to make San Francisco fall into the sea?'

'Exactly,' Luc said with a warm smile, and without warning he leaned over and kissed her cheek.

'You may mock,' Pascal said loudly, 'but you mark my words. It will come, and when it does, you'll be sorry.'

'And you're gonna be sorry in the morning, Pascal, when your head hurts from all the beers you've been drinking. Off home with you now,' Francie said with mock crossness. She placed the dented metal tray she had been carrying down on the table and started to clear the empty bottles.

'And I don't know what you two are grinning about. You should be off as well. Nurse Jenny is still recovering, and you've got patients to see in the morning.' Francie shooed them off with a wave of her dishcloth.

'I think that's our cue,' Luc said, standing up. Jenny joined him and swayed a little, deciding that she should have paid more attention to what she was drinking, and at some point have switched to water as Luc had done after his one and only beer. With Luc's arm around her waist and cupping her elbow, she made it to the Jeep without injuring or embarrassing herself.

'Thanks for tonight,' she said as she climbed into the passenger seat with some effort. 'Just what I needed.'

Luc chuckled. 'It's good to see you let your hair down. You're here on holiday, but I think you have worked more than you have relaxed.'

'All that's going to change,' Jenny said, looking at him and trying to blink away some of the alcohol-induced fatigue. 'Doctor's orders?' she asked with a smile, and Luc smiled back.

As they drove along the road that wound around the edge of the island, Jenny could both hear and see that the wind had picked up. The waves were crashing on the beach with an increasing frequency, and the wind was buffeting the Jeep.

'Are you sure Pascal's not right about this?' Jenny said, sitting up straighter in her seat and peering out into the darkness. 'It's pretty rough out there.'

'Relax, Jenny, it's just the tail-end of a storm. By the morning, we'll be back to clear skies and calm waters. The weather's like that out here: it blows up as quickly as it passes.'

Jenny knew that Luc was probably right — he had lived on the island for most of his childhood, after all — but her experience of island weather so far warned her that her gut feeling might just be right. Luc seemed unaffected by the conditions, and just calmly corrected the course of the Jeep whenever a gust of wind hit. They pulled up in front of the shack just as a large piece of corrugated steel blew past them like paper in a breeze.

'You were saying?' Jenny asked, her fear cutting through the tiredness and the beer.

'Relax. It's probably not even from the shack. I'll check it's safe before I go.'

Jenny got out of the Jeep. That wasn't exactly what she had meant. The wind was whipping around her now, and she pulled her cardigan tightly round herself.

'Go and check if you have power. If not, you might want to come back with me.'

Jenny could just about make out the words over the howl of the wind. She unlocked the door and clicked the switch, and the light came on. For a brief moment she wasn't all that sure she was glad it had. The thought was lost when she glanced upwards and realised she could see the sky — or at least the blackness of the outside.

'Damn,' she said to herself as she went back outside to find Luc.

'There's a hole in the roof!' she shouted when she saw him pulling a sheet of flat wood around the side.

'I know. I'll fix this over it, and make sure someone comes out to do a proper job in the morning.' Luc positioned a rickety ladder up against the side of the shack.

'Luc, stop. It's too dangerous. Maybe I should go back to Francie's — we can come back and fix it tomorrow when the weather's settled.'

'All your stuff will get wet, and that's assuming the local wildlife doesn't decide to move in. Won't take me a minute.'

And before she could answer he had started to climb the ladder, pulling the sheet of wood behind him. She sighed, knowing that there was nothing she could say to change what he was about to do, and moved so she could support some of the wooden sheet's weight.

Then the weight was gone, and there was the faint sound of nails being hammered.

'I'm coming down!' Luc shouted, and his feet appeared over the edge of the roof. 'Go back inside! You're going to get soaked!'

And, as if Luc had a direct line to the weather gods, the heavens opened and it rained. Not rain like in England, but huge, heavy drops that stung when they hit bare flesh. Jenny pulled her cardigan over her head and turned to make her way towards the light spilling from the inside of the shack. There was a crack, the light went out, and then the sound of splintering wood ripped through the air — followed by a dull thud.

15

Jenny spun on her heel and listened, sure of what she had heard but unable to make out anything in the sudden blackness. She stumbled in the direction of the noise where she thought she would find Luc, having fallen from the roof.

'Luc?' she shouted, trying to keep panic from her voice. 'Luc?!'

There was no sound, or at least none she could make out over the wind. It was probably her panicked imagination, but she was sure that the weather had increased in fierceness in the few moments since she had last seen him. She felt frantically for the side of the shack to give her some sort of reference point in the darkness, and then used it to guide herself around the building. Within moments she was soaked to the skin, and couldn't tell if it was the rain running down her cheeks or tears.

'Luc?' she called, again trying to ignore the old adage that those who were quiet were more likely to be seriously injured than those who were screaming.

'Here . . .' a muted voice called. Jenny continued towards the direction of the sound, and when her foot struck something solid she stopped, crouching down and feeling for what she had hit. Her hand touched a smashed piece of wood — either part of the roof or the ladder, she wasn't sure. She placed it carefully to one side, and on her hands and knees felt the ground around it until she found where Luc lay. She thought she could hear a groan as she realised she was touching an arm. She moved slightly, and could just about make out his face in the gloom.

'Where does it hurt?'

'Everywhere.' Luc seemed to be having trouble breathing out. With expert hands, Jenny started to run a secondary survey, having to rely on what she could feel and touch since she could see so little. She ran her hands around the back of Luc's head and was relieved to feel nothing out of the ordinary. She moved on to his face.

'Not that I'm not enjoying this . . . ' she heard him say as she moved to check his neck and shoulders. ' . . . but I just winded myself. Perhaps we could continue this indoors, out of the rain?'

Jenny had to fight the urge to punch him on the shoulder, her fear that he had been seriously injured starting to fade.

'I'm not sure you should move. You fell over six feet; the risk of spinal injury is real.' She had to lean down close to his face to make herself heard.

'I fell off the ladder, only a couple of feet. My back's fine, I just knocked all the air out my lungs.'

At that, Luc pushed himself up on his elbows with another groan, and then rolled onto his knees. Jenny hooked an arm around his shoulder, and between them they got him to his feet.

Completely disorientated, with rain lashing at her face, Jenny realised that she had no idea which way the door to the shack was. They staggered together in what they thought was the right way, but ended up walking the long way round until Jenny's hand touched on a gap in the wall. By feel alone, she helped Luc over to the bed and sat him on the edge before she returned to the spot where she had left the candles and matches in case the power went out. She lit one, double-checked that the door was closed and latched, and headed back to look over Luc. On a quick visual check, she could see no signs of bleeding or bruising.

'I'm fine, Jenny, really. Although I'm happy for you to run your hands over me again if you'd like.'

Now Jenny did slap him lightly on the arm, and he rolled away, holding it in mock pain.

'What was that for?' he asked in pretend indignation.

'For scaring me,' she said, glaring at

him. 'And for being cheeky.'

'I just fell off your roof trying to fix it for you!'

'You just fell off a *ladder*, and you get no sympathy from me. I told you to leave it, but you didn't listen.'

'Well, I suppose that's true . . . but don't I win any points for being a hero?'

'You lose points for being an idiot.' She turned away, as she knew she wasn't going to be able to keep the smile from her face. In truth, it was nice to be taken care of instead of being the one doing the caring. It wasn't that she didn't love her job, it was just pleasant to feel like someone was watching out for her instead.

She walked over to the tiny cooker and managed to light the gas. 'Tea?'

'Please, and then I should be going.'

Jenny turned to stare at him.

'Out there? In this? I don't think so.' She dumped a couple of teabags into the teapot. 'You have a short memory for what happened on my first night here.' The images of that night started to play in her head, and she shook it to try and dislodge them. She didn't want to remember.

'Are you okay if I stay?' The voice came from right beside her, and made Jenny jump as she was suddenly aware of his closeness.

'You can't go out in that, so we don't have much choice.'

Luc was studying her closely, and so she turned away to concentrate on pouring hot water into the teapot.

'Okay,' he said, 'but no funny business.'

Jenny rolled her eyes, and even though she had her back to him, she felt sure he knew.

'Hey, you were the one who made the first move last time,' he said with an innocent air.

She handed him a cup and gave him a hard stare.

'Alright, no need to be like that. I can sleep on the floor.'

'You just fell off the roof . . . '

'Ladder,' Luc corrected her, and she

glared at him again.

'Whatever: you just fell flat on your back from a height. I don't think sleeping on the floor is going to make you feel any better in the morning. You can sleep in the bed. We're both adults; I'm sure we can keep to our own sides.' She took a sip of tea, hoping to hide the blush that she knew was forming on her face; but the tea was too hot and made her wince, knowing she had just burnt her tongue.

'Careful. It's hot,' Luc said, his eyes dancing with amusement.

Jenny disappeared into the bathroom and pulled on her shortie pyjamas that had Disney characters plastered all over them. Before she had left, she had decided that comfort was the name of the game since she wasn't anticipating any romance, and so she had ditched the slinky numbers she had originally bought for the occasion. Now she was wishing she had gone for something a bit more mature.

She stared at her reflection in the

cracked mirror. It was hard to make out much in the candlelight, but she could see enough to know that she looked like a twelve-year-old girl at a sleepover. *It's a good thing*, she told herself firmly. *You know you're not ready to move on.* The pyjamas might just be the thing they both needed. Without thinking of how she would find the bed, she blew out the candle, hoping that she could slip under the blanket without being seen in all her glory.

She walked back into the main room and lifted the covers so she could slide into bed. Luc had left his candle burning, and once she was settled she heard him blow it out. She lay on her back for a while, getting used to not being alone in her bed once more, and then turned on her side.

'Do you want to snuggle?' a voice said.

'No!' Jenny said indignantly. 'We're adults, remember; not teenagers at our first boy-girl sleepover.'

'It's pretty scary weather out there,'

he added, and Jenny lay still for a few moments listening to the storm batter the island. 'I'll be the perfect gentleman, I promise.'

Jenny's resolve faded in mere moments, and she rolled over into Luc's arms which were ready to receive her. She could feel his quiet chuckle rumbling in his chest, and she knew that he had been certain he would win her over.

'Oh, stop it,' she whispered into his chest before falling asleep, feeling safe in his arms, like she had found her home.

* * *

There was a buzzing, and Jenny woke, wondering if Luc hummed in his sleep.

'What's that?' she said. It was dark, and the weather continued to rage outside. She had no idea how long she had been asleep, but it certainly wasn't morning yet. Luc held her tight with one arm, but she felt him move slightly to reach towards the wooden chair that

211

served as a bedside table.

'Pager,' he said. 'Mobile phones tend to be the first things to go in bad weather.'

The screen lit up the space around his hand as he pressed the button. 'Damn it!' he whispered, as if he was afraid of waking someone.

Jenny lifted her head from his chest so that she could read the screen. 'Who is it?' she murmured, not recognising the number.

'The clinic, and it's the emergency number. The equivalent of a 999 call. I'm going to have to go.' He kissed her on the head, then eased his arm out from underneath her and rolled out of bed. Before he could turn round, Jenny was out of bed too.

'I'll come. You might need an extra pair of hands.'

'You're on holiday, remember? An actual vacation, not a working one.'

There was a rumbling crash, and the sound of yawing wood.

'On second thoughts, you probably

should come,' Luc said, lighting his candle and shining it up towards the repaired roof. The makeshift patch was lifting up in the wind. 'I think you'll be safer at Francie's.' He turned to Jenny, but realised she had disappeared back into the bathroom with a handful of clothes.

'Ready,' Jenny said. He shook his head, and she knew he was torn between getting her to stay away from anything to do with work, and the need to keep her safe. She grinned as she knew that her safety would win him over; she had him pegged on that front, at least. Luc held out a hand and she took it, bracing themselves as they opened the door.

Although it was only feet away, they could barely make out the Jeep, through the rain and the sandstorm that was raging. They had to lean into the wind to make it to the door, and it took Jenny two attempts to open it against the gale's opposing strength. Luc turned the engine over, and the headlights of the Jeep lit up the scene. A row of palm trees had been uprooted and discarded like a toddler with toy cars.

Jenny gasped. 'Do you think Pascal was right?'

'Maybe,' Luc said as he turned the vehicle out onto the road. 'The tail-ends of tropical storms can be pretty fierce.'

The windscreen wipers were going-double time, barely keeping the smaller debris and lashing rain from the windscreen. Both Luc and Jenny leaned forward in their seats, and more than once Jenny called out that something was in the road just quick enough for Luc to take evasive manoeuvres. The journey seemed to take hours, and Jenny thought that they would never get there — at least, not in one piece.

When they arrived at the edge of the small town, Luc hit the brakes so quickly that Jenny barely had time to brace herself against the dashboard. Peering into the limited light from the Jeep headlights, she instantly knew why.

The clinic looked as if it had been sawn in half by a chainsaw. The roof was completely gone, and one wall had been split in two by what looked like a car.

16

Luc was out of the Jeep before Jenny's brain could process what she was seeing. All she could do was stare at the clinic. The slam of Luc's door was like a slap to her face and brought her back to her senses. Luc seemed frozen in place, and she followed his gaze as she realised that the whole row of property had been hit — including Francie's bar.

'There are torches in the back of the Jeep, and my medical kit.' Luc turned to her and she could see the anguish in his eyes. 'We'll need to set up a triage point. See if you can find somewhere with shelter?'

She reached out and squeezed his hand. She looked him in the eye, and although no words passed between them they were in perfect agreement. They had to do all they could to help their friends.

Jenny grabbed a torch and a lantern from the back of the Jeep, and started to walk slowly down the street, fighting against the wind which felt like it was buffeting her on every side; scanning for people, but also for somewhere safe to bring the wounded. None of the buildings had roofs anymore; most of them seemed to have collapsed in on themselves, or else been flattened by trees and other debris. Jenny had seen destruction on this scale on television, but never in real life. She felt almost hollow inside, as if her ability to feel anything else at all had disappeared.

Jenny turned away from the buildings and shone the torch across the stretch of beach. There was no sign now of any chairs or tables, or of the small bar that sat near the water's edge. Further up the beach, nestled between two leaning trees, the shed that housed the beach furniture appeared intact. Jenny jogged towards it, hoping it would provide shelter, hoping that there would be survivors. The sheet-metal door was latched, but there was no sign of any lock. She pulled it open and shone her torch inside. All four walls and the roof seemed to be in place. The floor had pools of water, and it was not exactly clean, but under the circumstances it would have to do. She placed the lantern on a table, and started to unstack chairs.

There was a noise, and Jenny froze: it sounded like a call for help, but she couldn't quite fix on its position. She stepped out of her relative shelter and turned her head into the wind, trying to listen for the sound above all the other noises. She grabbed the torch and made her way back to the Jeep. Luc was there, and he was not alone. Two men were carrying a still form, lying on what used to be a door.

'It's Cynthia,' Luc said. 'We found her just inside the clinic. She has a head wound. Did you find somewhere to triage?'

Jenny nodded. 'The shed for the beach stuff.'

'I'll send the injured to you. Do the best you can. Send for me if they're red. You know what to do if there are any code black?'

He looked up from his examination of Cynthia, and Jenny held his gaze for a split second. She had been involved in major incidents before, so she knew what the codes meant. She'd never had to classify patients herself, though. Code black meant clinically dead: individuals who in normal circumstances they would have tried to revive; but, in a situation like this when they had multiple casualties, they couldn't afford to waste time on. Time that could be better spent saving more lives than attempting to revive someone who was already gone and they were unlikely to get back.

'Jenny?'

'Yes, of course.' She turned to the men who held the makeshift stretcher. 'This way.'

Jenny grabbed the emergency medical kit from the back of the Jeep, and they made their way to the makeshift shelter. It was not easy battling the wind, and at one point Jenny was sure that the gusts would catch the door and spill its patient.

'Over here.' She directed the men to lay the door down in one corner, knowing that she would need to make room for more casualties. 'We're going to roll her,' she instructed her assistants. 'You might need the door for others.' Together, they carefully rolled Cynthia off the door and onto the ground.

'Go,' Jenny ordered them; they seemed overwhelmed by the sight of Cynthia lying so still, with blood pouring from the gash that ran raggedly across her forehead.

'Is she . . . ?' The man didn't finish his sentence.

'No,' Jenny said firmly. 'She's unconscious but she will be fine.' She shuddered slightly: there was no way to tell if that was actually the case. 'Go, please — help Luc.'

The men picked up the door and sped away. Jenny grabbed the medical kit and opened it, quickly pulling out all she needed. With practised hands, she cleaned the wounds and fixed a pressure bandage in place. Gently lifting up Cynthia's eyelids, she shone the torch into each eye in turn, checking for a reaction. To her relief, both pupils responded, which was a good sign, for now. She righted another table and emptied out the bag — without knowing how bad the casualties were, it made sense to have all the equipment where she could get to it fast.

One of the men now returned, holding up a woman of about Jenny's age with one arm, and in his other carrying what looked like a pile of blankets.

'The baby,' the man gasped as he managed to hand over the bundle before losing his grip on the woman. He sat her down against one wall. 'Doctor Luc says, cuts, bruises and shock. He says, baby cold but fine. I found some blankets.'

'Thank you,' Jenny said to his retreating back as he disappeared back to the disaster area. She cradled the baby and pulled out a digital thermometer which she placed under the infant's armpit. Luc was right: the baby was cold but alert. She knelt down in front of the woman.

'My name is Jenny. What's yours?' she asked, but the woman looked at her blankly, as if no words had been spoken. 'Is this your baby?' she tried again. At that moment, the baby let out a cry, which seemed to jerk the woman out of her shock just a little. The woman managed a nod, and her eyes focused on the baby. The thermometer beeped. Jenny read it and smiled reassuringly at the young mother.

'Baby's a little cold. The best way to warm her up is to hold her skin-to-skin.' Jenny quickly unwrapped the baby from her bundle of blankets and placed her against the woman's chest, inside her thin t-shirt.

'Now we need to keep you both warm,' she said, before wrapping the woman and her baby back up in the blankets — save for one, which she used to cover Cynthia's still form.

More casualties arrived, but Jenny was relieved to note that, apart from a couple of broken bones, there were no serious injuries. The shed was filling up, and the increased number of people meant that the air temperature inside was slowly starting to warm. The wind continued to howl, but Jenny was certain it was losing strength — maybe they would get through this. When Francie appeared, covered in dust and dirt but with no serious injuries, Jenny could have wept with relief. The two women hugged, but Jenny could tell that something was not right.

'It's okay, Francie, you're safe now.'

Francie pulled back, but gripped Jenny's upper arms.

'Jocelyn . . . ' she said with a voice full of agony. 'She went off to spend the night at a friend's. I can't find my phone.'

'The phones are out. Jocelyn will be fine, I'm sure.' Jenny said.

'I should never have let her go. We knew there was a storm coming. What was I thinking?'

Francie turned and started to pace, the anxiety radiating from her. Jenny caught up to her and grabbed one of her hands in an attempt to make her stand still.

'Francie, she's probably safer away. The bar collapsed, remember? When it's daylight I'll take you, I promise. But now you need to rest. You've been through an ordeal.'

Jenny gently pulled her to a seat, and Francie folded into it; but no sooner had Jenny turned away than Francie was on her feet again, pacing. The young mother who had seemed so shocked earlier had recovered enough to help Jenny, who turned to her now.

'Could you sit with Francie? And keep an eye on the others? I'm going to check on Luc,' Jenny said.

As Jenny stepped outside, she could see a thin strip of light on the horizon — a promise, it seemed, that, despite the events of the night before, the sun would still rise. There were more people helping now; clearly, word had spread. A pickup truck held bottles of water and other supplies. Luc was directing men and women, and didn't notice her approach.

'How's it going?' she asked, handing him a bottle of water from the back of the truck. He took it from her as if he had forgotten that he needed to drink, and swallowed half of it in one gulp. Water dribbled down his chin, and he wiped it away with a bloodstained hand.

'Are you hurt?'

'It's just a scratch,' he said with a shrug as if he were seeing it for the first time.

'It's more than that,' Jenny said, examining the jagged edges of the wound which ran across the back of his hand to his wrist. 'It needs cleaning and a dressing. Things get infected quickly in this climate.' She arched an eyebrow at him now, and his sigh told her that he remembered using the same words on her to make her stay after she had been injured trying to rescue Salomen.

'I need to stay here in case anyone else is found injured.' His look dared her to argue, and she knew she wouldn't win.

'Fine, the first aid will come to you,' Jenny said, turning on her heel to go and collect some supplies.

When she returned, she made Luc sit in the front seat of the Jeep. The indoor light and her torch meant that she could clearly see his injuries.

'We have to stop meeting like this,' he said to her, and she looked up at him and rolled her eyes.

'Really? That's the best you can do?'

'Post-incident humour at its best.'

Jenny taped the bandage in place. Luc raised an eyebrow. 'Not bad, Nurse

Jenny, but what if I need to treat a patient? I can't do it one-handed.'

Jenny raised a finger, indicating that she hadn't finished. She pulled a plastic glove from her pocket, pulled it onto his hand, and then taped the open end in place around his wrist. 'There. Now you can keep your wound clean and dry, and use anti-bac gel on the glove between patients.'

'There really is no end to your talents,' he said, and lifted up his good hand to hers before giving it a squeeze.

'I'm glad you said that. Can I borrow the Jeep?'

Luc's face looked questioning, but he said nothing.

'Francie is beside herself over Jocelyn. I want to drive her out to the friend's place where Jocelyn's staying.'

Luc shook his head. 'Too dangerous right now, and I need you here to monitor the patients.'

'What about Jocelyn?'

'I'll take Francie myself.'

Now it was Jenny's turn to raise an

eyebrow; that, and fold her arms over her chest.

'And the difference between *me* going and being in danger, and *you*, is . . . ?'

'It's down to a calculation of risk versus benefit. Everyone here is stable enough for you to look after. If we are going out of town, we are likely to find more injured people, and they might need a doctor.'

Jenny knew he was right, but that didn't mean she had to like it. She stared at him for a moment, torn between wanting to relieve Francie's anxiety and find Jocelyn, and the desire to keep Luc safe.

'Fine,' she said at last. 'Are we sure that we have everyone out from here?' She indicated the collapsed and destroyed buildings.

'As sure as we can be. The others will keep looking. I'll take Francie, and be back as soon as we can.'

He stood up, hesitated, and then pulled her into a quick, tight hug.

'Look after yourself,' he whispered, before releasing her so that he could lift her chin and kiss her full on the mouth. They broke apart as they had before, breathless and fighting the desire to continue.

'You're the one that needs to be careful.'

'Relax, Jenny, I know what I'm doing. I know these roads like I know my own mind,' Luc said. His quick wink was not lost on Jenny, nor was his meaning. She shook her head in exasperation, but all she could do was watch him drive away in the Jeep with Francie at his side.

17

The sun was high in the sky, and Jenny had not had to work hard to stay busy. More and more people had heard about the clinic, and had arrived to help and bring supplies. The weather had calmed, and if Jenny hadn't have lived through the night before, she wouldn't have believed it had happened. The sea was rolling gently onto the beach, and the sky was as blue as she had imagined the Caribbean would be. She was glad she wasn't wearing a watch, knowing that she would be counting every minute until Luc returned. She wasn't sure why she was so worried. The storm had passed, and all he was doing was driving a few miles down the road to the small former plantation property where Jocelyn's friend lived. What could be safer? But still Jenny couldn't keep from her mind the nagging thought that something was going to go wrong.

A car drove up and parked at an angle. Jenny instantly recognised it as Armand's. She hurried towards it, wondering if it held yet more casualties, and at the same time worrying at how few medical supplies they had left, the other supplies having been buried under the collapsed building that used to be the clinic. Armand climbed out, mercifully looking all in one piece.

'Nurse Jenny,' he said by way of greeting.

'Armand, are you alright?'

'Take more than a bit of wind to take me out.' He smiled broadly, and Jenny found herself pulled into a hug. 'Looks like you and Doctor Luc got things up and running,' he said, with a nod in the direction of the new temporary clinic. 'Speaking of which, where is the Doc?'

'Took Francie to go find Jocelyn. She was staying at a friend's last night.'

Armand tilted his head to one side. 'That she was, which is why I went to get her. Figured Francie would be worried sick. Joe told me she was okay even if the bar's not. Thought the best I could do was reunite 'em. I know what my sister's like.'

Jenny felt like her blood had frozen in its veins as she peered into the car and could make out the sleeping Jocelyn lying across the back seat.

'She okay?' Jenny asked, concerned.

'Just worn out. Her and her friends stayed up all night to watch the storm. Teenagers,' Armand added, with a sniff of both disgust and Unclely love.

'You didn't see Luc's Jeep on the way?' Jenny asked, trying to stay calm, and ignoring her inner voice which was screaming *Told you so!*

'No.' Armand's eyes had drifted to the bar. He let out a whistle. 'That's going to take some fixing up.'

Jenny reached out a hand for his arm, needing him to give her his full attention.

'Armand, is there any other way to this friend's house?'

He shook his head.

'Aren't that many roads on this island, Nurse Jenny.'

'Then where are they?' Jenny almost shouted, and Armand held up both hands as if to keep her at bay.

'Knowing Doctor Luc and Francie . . . helping folks. Likely there's a lot that need help right now.'

Jenny shook her head, knowing she couldn't ignore her inner voice any longer.

'No, no, there's something wrong.'

'What's wrong?' a voice said, and Jenny turned in surprise. Cynthia was up, walking and talking and looking every bit her old self except for the bandage around her head. 'All this your doing, Nurse Jenny?' she asked with a smile.

Jenny nodded impatiently. 'Luc and Francie went off to fetch Jocelyn, but Armand collected her and he didn't see them on the way. I think something's wrong.'

'Most likely helping people. Doctor

Luc always works himself to the bone.'

Jenny knew that she wasn't going to get far like this. 'Armand, can I borrow your car?'

Now both Cynthia and Armand were looking at her as if she were the one with the head injury.

'To go where? Looking for Francie and Doctor Luc? I'm telling you, Nurse Jenny, they'll be fine.'

'Will you be alright here?' Jenny turned, ignoring Armand, to look at Cynthia, who nodded. She held out her hand to Armand in a gesture that was clearly asking for the keys. Armand shook his head, and Jenny was beginning to formulate a different plan, when he spoke:

'If you're going, then I'm coming with you.'

Jenny opened her mouth to argue; but if Luc was in trouble, then she could probably use an extra pair of hands. She climbed into the car and waited as Armand shook Jocelyn awake and handed her over to Cynthia's care.

Armand climbed into the driving seat and Cynthia handed Jenny a plastic bag which contained some of the remaining medical supplies. Jenny opened her mouth to argue, but Cynthia's look said it all. They were doing okay at the new clinic, but Jenny might find a completely different set of circumstances once she explored more of the island.

They drove in silence. Jenny had nothing she could think of to say, other than to worry out loud about Luc and Francie, and Armand seemed content to leave her to her thoughts. At last he pulled the car over opposite a dusty lane that led uphill. In the distance, Jenny could make out an older wooden building with a wide porch. The paint was peeling, but otherwise it seemed well-cared-for, and certainly unaffected by the storm.

'That's it,' Armand said, gesturing in that direction.

'So where are they?' Jenny replied.

'Maybe someone flagged them down.

The Doc's Jeep is well-known in these parts.'

'But who would be out here?' Jenny gestured to the surrounding area. There were no other buildings, or even side roads, that she could see.

'They're probably back at the clinic, drinking tea — like we could be,' he said gloomily. 'It's been a long night, Nurse Jenny, and I'm beat. 'Spect you are too.'

Jenny couldn't feel anything but concern. She knew she should be tired, but she was numb to it. She would sleep when she found Luc safe and well. Maybe they would even pick up where they had left off. What was it he'd called it? *Snuggling* . . .

The memory of being held by Luc did nothing to ease her concern, and in fact made her more determined. She pushed open the car door and made to step out.

'Where you going?' Armand asked, one hand on her arm.

'I think they're out there, and I'm

going to find them.'

'What you gonna do? Just keep walking till you fall over 'cause of the heat? You ain't even got water.'

'I know you think I'm crazy, but I just know something's wrong.'

Armand sighed.

'Close the door. Francie'd have my head if she thought I'd let you go wandering by yourself.'

Jenny gave him a quick, tight smile.

'If they got flagged down, they must have gone that way.' Jenny indicated ahead. 'If they doubled back, we would have seen them pass the clinic.'

With one more look in her direction — that Jenny suspected was to see if there was any chance her mind could be changed — Armand turned the key, and they made their way further on up the road. It wound tightly, and Jenny knew that they were headed up into the centre of the island, away from the beaches.

'Do many people live up here?' she asked.

'Not many; most live by the water. The main town's on the other side — where we arrived, you know?'

Jenny scanned her surroundings, looking for any sign of the Jeep, but there was nothing — or, at least, nothing she could detect in the crushed and wind-trampled undergrowth. Trees and large ferns had been uprooted, causing the tightly-packed forest to appear even more impenetrable. The further they travelled, the more hopeless Jenny felt it was going to be. There was no way they would find Luc and Francie, particularly if they had come off of the road. They needed the helicopter, but she suspected that would be kept busy ferrying patients to the mainland.

The car slowed and then stopped. Armand opened his door and stepped out, studying something on the road. Jenny joined him but could make out nothing unusual about the sandy road and decimated forest that surrounded them.

'What is it?' Jenny asked, scanning around them.

Armand pointed off and up, into the forest, and Jenny followed his gaze. It was then that she saw it, despite the fact that the forest seemed to have almost swallowed it up. The Jeep, perched at an impossible angle, suspended between trees, dangerously near the edge that hung high above the lower winding road.

Jenny lurched forward, but Armand grabbed her around the waist.

'No, Nurse Jenny. The whole hillside is unstable — look at the water running.'

The voice made her focus. She could see water running from the hills above them, across the road, and on down the hill where the Jeep had settled.

'Doctor Luc? Francie?' Armand called, and Jenny could hear the fear in his voice. 'Answer me!'

'Here,' a voice called, sounding like it was coming from a distance.

'Francie?' Armand shouted. Now it

was his turn to rush forward, but Jenny stayed him by grabbing his arm.

'Francie. Can you tell us where you are?' Jenny shouted.

'I got out. Wanted to get help, but I'm stuck.'

Jenny's blood ran cold. If Francie had got out to summon help, what did that mean for Luc?

'Francie, we can't see you in the brush,' Armand called. 'Can you wave something, make some noise?'

Armand and Jenny stood still, scanning the forest for any sign of her. Then Jenny gripped Armand's arm and pointed. 'There,' she said. 'Over there.' Without exchanging words, they both headed in the direction of the branch they could see waving. Jenny slipped and slid in the mud, and Armand caught her before she built up so much momentum that she would keep going down the slick side of the hill. They scrambled over downed trees and tangled vines which scratched at their legs and arms, but neither of them felt a thing. Francie was barely visible, one arm wrapped around a tree root that was bending under her weight.

'Don't come no closer, you'll fall,' Francie begged.

Jenny looked around for something fixed to hold on to, cursing the fact that they hadn't brought anything useful with them like rope.

'Here,' she said, pulling a vine from a tree. She did notice the pain this time as it bit into the palm of her hand. 'Tie this around your waist.'

Armand took the end of the vine and, without taking his eyes off his sister, lashed it around his middle. He turned to look at her. Jenny ran her end of the vine around a tree that was still standing, then wrapped it around her own waist and braced herself.

'Go, I've got you,' she said to Armand, who didn't hesitate, but practically threw himself in the direction of his sister.

The moments ticked by in agonising slowness as Jenny watched Armand slip and fall before picking himself back up. When he reached Francie, she watched as brother and sister embraced, and Jenny heard Armand share the news that she knew Francie wanted above anything else.

'Jocelyn is safe, Francie. I went to get her myself.'

That was all Francie needed to know. She threw herself into her brother's arms, and Jenny could hear her sob.

'Come, come,' Armand said, not unkindly. 'We have to get you out of here so Nurse Jenny can get you fixed up.'

'I can't move; my ankle is twisted.'

'Then I will carry you. Put your arms around my neck.'

Jenny felt the tension on the vine increase, and locked her knees, preparing to take the weight of them both if she needed to. Armand made slow progress back towards her, and whilst she was deeply grateful that Francie was alright, her mind kept playing scenarios of what might have happened to Luc. Why hadn't he been the one to go for help? Sending Francie up a dangerously unstable cliffside was not something that he would have done lightly. Not something he would have done unless he could not go himself — which meant he was hurt, most likely seriously.

The pull on her end of the vine increased, and almost caught Jenny by surprise; she had to lean her full weight back as her trainers looked for purchase on the ground that was slick with running water. Armand struggled to maintain his balance, and for a terrifying moment Jenny thought that both he and his sister would fall — but, with muscles straining, he managed to redress his balance, and continue his slow way back to where Jenny stood in relative safety.

When he reached her, he gently set Francie down on the ground. Jenny knelt down and began a quick survey of the other woman's injuries; finally reaching Francie's ankle, which was twice the size that it should be, and dark with bruising under the skin. Jenny gently unlaced the shoe to reduce the tight pressure on it, and was rewarded with a hissed intake of breath from Francie.

'Sorry. It may be broken, so you shouldn't walk on it. We should leave your shoe on to act as a splint.' Jenny finally allowed herself to look the other woman in the eye. 'Francie, where's Luc? What happened?'

'The other car. It swerved off the road and down the hill. It was going to fall, and we couldn't get the people out. Luc attached the towing cable from the Jeep to it, but it was too heavy and the wheels couldn't get traction. It pulled him over. I tried to get down there to help him, but my ankle . . . ' She trailed off, gesturing at it. 'I couldn't get to him, and I couldn't get back up.'

Jenny clenched her hands to stop them from shaking. She knew what she had to do.

'Francie, we have to get you back to

the clinic and get that ankle seen to. Armand, help me,' she instructed as she hauled Francie up to stand on her one good ankle, and slung her arm around the woman's shoulder. Armand repeated the move on Francie's other side, and between them they half-carried her back up to Armand's car.

'We need to go and get help. No way we can get to Doctor Luc without more hands.'

Jenny grabbed the carry bag full of supplies, and slammed the door on the passenger side now that Francie was safely inside.

'Go,' she said, turning away.

'You have to come too,' Armand said, and his eyes flashed a warning.

'I need to stay here and see if I can get to Luc.'

'It's too dangerous; we need ropes and heavy trucks. Look what happened to Francie.'

'I have to try,' Jenny said, and headed back into the forest before Armand could make a move to stop her. She could hear him calling her name; deep down, she knew that he was probably right. The sensible thing to do was to wait for further help — but there was no way she was going to just stand around for what could be valuable minutes of Luc's life ticking away.

18

Jenny wasn't sure if Armand had stopped shouting her name and headed off to fetch help, or if the forest was acting like a soundproof barrier. She swung the bag of supplies over one shoulder, and with the help of the vine managed to make her way back to where they had found Francie — but she still couldn't make out the Jeep, let alone the other car which had gone spinning off the road. She was covered in mud, with tiny cuts to her face, arms and legs, but none of it mattered or even registered. She had to get to Luc. With one arm wrapped firmly around a tree, she took a moment to get her breath back, and tried to work out the safest route down.

There was movement to her right and she froze, thoughts of what might be out there cutting through the fear for

Luc which had been driving her onwards with no thought to her own safety. As quickly as it was there, it was gone . . . but something else caught her eye. A flash of something — the light of a mirror, perhaps? She headed in that direction, her desire to reach it overcoming her careful steps. Soon she felt her feet slide from under her, and she was tumbling downwards — fast.

The path she was hurtling down seemed free from debris and large trees, and her hands felt bumps in the sodden mud's tyre-tracks. Jenny reached out to try and slow her descent, but only succeeded in adding to lacerations on her hands and arms. The rear of the Jeep suddenly lurched into view, and Jenny crashed into it shoulder-first. The breath was knocked out of her and she forced herself to stay still, terrified that her actions might be all that was needed to force the Jeep back into its downward skid. The vehicle rocked, and the sound of stressed metal squealed through the forest like the noise of arguing monkeys.

'Hold still. It's okay. We're not going anywhere, I promise.'

Luc's voice! Jenny could feel tears burning in her eyes as a sense of relief swept through her. One of the basics of first aid was that people who could talk were breathing, which meant they were alive. She leaned over the side of the Jeep to see if she could pinpoint where Luc's voice was. Through the side rear window, she could tell that the Jeep was empty. Luc wasn't there, and that meant two things. Firstly, he wasn't so badly injured that he couldn't move; and secondly, he was likely trying to help the occupants of the second car.

Making her movements slow and precise, Jenny hauled herself down so that her feet were resting on the open Jeep door.

'Luc?' she called, knowing that she couldn't put it off any longer. She had to let him know that she was there, that she had come to help.

'Jenny? What the hell!'

In the past, Luc's anger had made her pause, but right now it felt like the best sound in the world.

'I'm coming down to you,' she said.

'Jenny, we're balanced precariously. Unless you have a tow rope attached to the Jeep, you need to stay where you are.'

Jenny shook her head. 'Help's on its way, and I have supplies.'

There was a pause, and Jenny knew that Luc was processing the information that she had climbed down the hillside without waiting for professional help. She seized the moment, knowing that if she waited his anger might be enough to hold her back, but right now she needed to see with her own eyes that he was alright. She looked for a foothold and moved, but the ground was too slick, and before she knew it she was sliding on one foot and her side. She made a frantic grab for something to slow her, and managed to catch the tow rope. Her hands were covered in mud, and she had to grip tight to stop herself, the rough metal digging into her already painful palms. She grunted with the effort and pain.

'Jenny?' There was less anger now, and more concern; although Jenny knew that, with Luc, the two emotions were closely linked. There was the sound of groaning metal, and Luc's face appeared out of the open rear car door.

'You're going to have to hand-over-hand it, like on the monkey bars when you were a kid.'

Jenny commanded her hands to move, but they refused to obey her.

'I'll catch you, I promise,' Luc said, but still Jenny couldn't move, as much as she wanted to be near enough to touch him.

'Jenny!' The voice was sharp now. 'You were foolish enough to put yourself in this position, now you've got to follow through. Move it! You're putting additional weight on the very thing keeping us where we are, and if you don't hurry you might kill us all!'

The shouting seemed to cut through the fear, and slowly one of Jenny's hands released its death grip and moved just a few inches. She stared at it as if it were obeying Luc's command rather than her own.

'That's it. Just like that; slow and steady.' There was an edge to his voice, but the anger was less, and the command seemed to strike through the barrier in Jenny's brain. One hand and then the other, one hand and then the other; all the while, her feet scrabbled to find purchase. Something gripped one foot, and in her panic she nearly kicked it away, fearing that she had fallen foul of some forest monster; but something stopped her just in time.

'I've got you, keep coming.'

With a few more movements, Luc had his arms wrapped tightly around her legs, and she could feel herself being pulled into the back seat of the car. She and Luc landed heavily, the car screamed against the tow rope, and

Jenny was spilled from Luc's grip into the seat-well. For a moment, no one spoke. They stayed still, as if they were playing a game of statues. Slowly, the rocking movement of the car subsided.

'What did you think you were doing?' Luc's voice was hard and flat as he moved slowly so that he was sat upright and could look down at Jenny, lying strewn across the two footwells.

'I thought you might need help with your patient,' Jenny said, knowing that he would be more angry if she told him the real reason. 'Cynthia gave me some supplies,' she added, wriggling so that she could release the plastic bag from its tie on her arm.

'You could have just attached the bag to a rope and let it down to me,' Luc said, and Jenny could see his jaw muscles clench as he worked to control his temper. 'All you've succeeded in doing is ensuring the professionals now have three people to rescue instead of two.'

Jenny's elbow was jammed under the

seat in front, so she moved a little to relieve the pressure. She could feel her own anger building now that the relief that Luc was okay was fading.

'And what did *you* think you were doing when you were playing the hero? How come it's okay for you to place yourself in danger, but everyone else has to do as you say?' She twisted again to try and move, but was well and truly stuck. Two hands reached for her and she was unceremoniously pulled up onto the seat alongside Luc.

'Why do you have an apparent death wish?' he demanded. 'I know you're recovering from an emotional trauma, but even so . . . This crazy behaviour has to stop.'

Jenny glared at him. Not only were his comments unfair, but they were also untrue. She had no desire to end it all; in fact, the break-up with Kai had only made her more determined to find what it was she wanted in life and to go after it, not letting anyone else stand in her way.

'Pot and kettle, Doctor. Pot and kettle.' Jenny knew she was being childish, but couldn't help herself. He was being infuriating, and surely this was not the place to have this conversation.

'Perhaps we should stick to the task at hand,' he said, and Jenny wondered if he could read her mind.

'Of course. What do you need?' She said the words in a cold, professional and detached manner. If he wanted to be all businesslike, so be it — she could play along.

'Sophia has a laceration to her right arm; severed the brachial artery. I made a temporary tourniquet, but I'd be happier to tie it off.'

Jenny opened the bag and pulled out a small surgical pack which contained sutures. 'Here. Did you get a line in?'

Luc took the pack and started to move over the handbrake into the front seat. 'Yes, but I've run through the bag of fluid I have.'

'I have half a litre of Hartman's. It's

not much, but it should buy us some more time.'

'Sophia,' Luc addressed his patient, all trace of anger gone from his voice. He was firmly back in doctor mode. 'Sophia, open your eyes.' Jenny couldn't see Sophia's face, but she judged that Luc had managed to get a response out of the woman.

'Sophia, I'm going to tie off the vessel that is bleeding, so I can release the tourniquet a little.'

'Hurts . . . ' Sophia said.

'I know; but if I can tie off the vessel, then I can relieve the pressure; it's that that is causing you the pain.'

Jenny waited, knowing that anything she had to say would distract Luc from a task that would be difficult enough in a hospital, let alone in a car suspended on the side of a hill. Not that she could think of much to say, anyway. All the things she could have said would be best saved for a time when their lives weren't in peril.

'Okay, that's done, Sophia. Now I'm

going to release the tourniquet a little.'

'Has the bleeding stopped?' Jenny asked.

'Slowed greatly. A couple of smaller vessels are still bleeding, but the imminent danger is over. Can you pass me the Hartman's?'

Jenny leaned forward with her hand outstretched; as she did so, the car started to move. Jenny froze, not daring even to breathe. The movement slowed, and then stopped, Jenny swallowed and tried again.

'Stop,' Luc said. 'Your weight must be acting as a counterbalance since the car last slipped. You need to stay in the back. Can you put the fluid in the bag and lower it through without moving too much?'

Jenny followed his instructions, and gently lowered the bag to a point that Luc could grab it. She waited for the car to move; but, other than a slight rock, it stayed in place. She let herself breathe again, and tried not to focus on how they were all going to get safely out when any movement from her could send them plunging to a dire end. She watched as Luc gently moved a hand across the gap between the seats to check Sophia's pulse. He seemed satisfied, and then brought his arm slowly back to his side.

'What are we going to do?' she whispered, knowing that Luc couldn't have any answers, but needing to hear his voice. She knew it was selfish in that moment, but she hoped that the anger was gone. She had tried to help, but realised deep down that she had probably made things worse — much worse.

'I don't know.' He craned his neck around the headrest so that he could see her. 'The mainland has probably sent help by now. Armand and Francie know where we are, so it shouldn't be too long.'

Jenny recognised the tone of voice, one that she had used many times to reassure a patient when the situation was bad. She wasn't sure if Luc was using it for her benefit or Sophia's; but despite the fact she recognised it, she found it comforting somehow.

'All we can do is sit tight and wait,' Luc said — and something heavy hit the car roof.

19

Sophia moaned, and the car shifted — but only a few centimetres.

'It's okay, it's okay,' Luc said, and Jenny saw him place a reassuring hand on the woman's arm. She could see him peer out of the front windscreen as he tried to work out what had happened.

Jenny moved towards the open rear door, being careful to ensure her weight stayed at the back of the vehicle. A luminous pouch swung from a bright orange rope. Jenny shifted again, aware that Luc could see her movements but not what she was reaching for.

'Careful,' he said softly, but there was no condemnation in his voice. Even though he couldn't see what she was doing, he seemed to instinctively trust her. Somehow, that seemed to make Jenny more nervous. She shifted again, waiting for a screech of metal;

but there was nothing except for a crackling noise. She stretched out her hand for the pouch, but couldn't quite reach it. Biting her lip, she tried again, and this time caught the swinging pouch between the tips of two fingers and carefully pulled it into the car. The rope gave as she pulled on it, so that she could sit herself in the centre of the back seat. She pulled the Velcro seal, and inside found a black hand-held radio.

'It's a radio,' she said to Luc, not sure if he could see from where he was sitting. A hand reached around the front seat, and Jenny placed the contraption into it.

'This is Doctor Luc Buchannan,' he said into the radio. There was a hiss as he released the button, and then a tinny voice could be heard.

'Doctor Luc. Good to hear your voice. I am Captain Renard, Fire and Rescue, flown in from the mainland. We don't have much of a visual — can you tell me what is going on down there?'

'Three souls. One injured, lacerated arm needing urgent medical treatment. We are in a car which is attached by a tow rope to a Jeep. Our position has changed several times. Any movement inside the car, and the whole thing shifts.'

'Understood, Doctor. We're going to work to secure the Jeep from up here. Then we should be able to get you out.'

'My patient doesn't have that kind of time, Captain. Can you send a simultaneous rescue team down for her?'

'Negative, Doctor. Until we can assess the state of the hillside, any movement might cause further slip — not to mention, removing that kind of weight from the car might tip the nose down, putting more pressure on the tow rope.'

'What about if I move to the back of the car once you retrieve my patient?'

Luc looked around at Jenny now, and she knew what he was asking. She nodded.

'It's risky, Doc.'

'Understood, but it's riskier to my patient if we leave her here.'

There was crackling over the radio, but no words were spoken.

'Your call, Doc. We'll secure the Jeep as quickly as possible, and my team will make their way up from the bottom of the ravine. Should reduce any movement of earth above you.'

'All received.'

To Jenny, it felt like hours before the hard-hatted heads appeared about a metre away from them. They moved slowly and deliberately, clearing their ropes every few steps.

'Doctor Buchannan? We're going to open the driver's-side door. We need you to move slowly through to the back seat. We have one tether on the Jeep; it should hold you for now, enough so you can shift to the back.'

Luc nodded and Jenny could hear that his breathing was heavy. She reached out an arm, but he shook his head in warning, and she took that as an indication that she should stay still.

There was not much room, and she had to fight the urge to move to make it easier. The cables groaned as the rescuers pulled Sophia from her seat. A head appeared at the window.

'Sit tight; we'll be back.'

Jenny and Luc both nodded, as if they were both afraid that speaking might cause sudden unwelcome movement.

'That was scary,' Jenny whispered. Luc reached out and squeezed her hand.

'Funny, 'cause you give the impression that all of these stunts are just run-of-the-mill to you.'

Jenny groaned inwardly. Apparently, they really were going to do this now.

'What can I say? I have a built-in instinct to help.'

'Even when that could get you killed?'

'Well, that thought process didn't seem to stop you. You know I wouldn't be down here if you hadn't rushed headlong into hero mode.'

'I'm no hero,' he said, in that all-too-familiar toneless voice.

'Okay, that's it. You need to tell me whatever it is that turns you into a robot with anger issues. And don't tell me you're just concerned about me, because I don't buy it. You only just met me, for a start.' Jenny leaned back a little and rested her head on the back of the seat. Luc looked away out of the window, as if he were tracking the progress of the rescue team, which Jenny knew by now would be well out of sight.

'You brought it up. If you don't want to talk about it, that's fine.' She knew she was goading him a little, but she needed to know. She suspected that if they weren't in this situation he would never tell her — she wasn't even sure he would tell her now. 'You know pretty much all my embarrassing dark secrets, so it's only fair that you share yours with me.'

She reached out for his hand and squeezed. He didn't squeeze back, but instead looked down at it and then pulled away.

'Luc, you've said that you like me. Well, I like you too, but this is never going to be more than it is now if you can't be honest with me, like I've been with you.'

'It's different for me.'

Jenny shook her head. 'Well, it can't be more embarrassing than realising the man you thought loved you really just saw you as financial security.' She was amazed at how she could say those words out loud without the familiar accompanying pain.

'It's not embarrassing, Jenny, it's shameful. None of what happened to you is your fault. You loved Kai, and so you trusted him and forgave the worst of him, which is what you are supposed to do if you love someone.'

'If you believe that to be true, then you need to tell me whatever it is, Luc. I know you and I trust you.'

'You don't know me!' His eyes flashed with pain and anger, but this time she was sure it was directed inwardly.

'My brother died, Jenny, and it was all my fault.'

Jenny could see all the muscles in Luc's face clench, and she knew he was trying to hold back the wave of emotion that he felt.

'I'm so sorry.' She reached out for him, but he pulled away so suddenly that the car jerked forward a few inches. Instinctively, they both grabbed for the handles inside the door and braced themselves. They jerked forward as the chain the rescuers had used to secure the Jeep took the strain. For a few moments, which felt like precious minutes to Jenny, it seemed as if one of the cables was going to give way. They could hear the scream of metal fatigue. A thought hit Jenny like she had been punched in the gut, stealing all the air from her lungs.

'What if the tow line can't take the strain?' she said; quietly, as if talking louder might endanger them further.

'It's coped so far, and I'm sure the rescuers have considered it.'

She looked at him, and could see the anger had faded, but still had no idea why he was so furious. It was common to feel angry when a loved one died, but this rage seemed directed both out to the world and inward as well.

'I shouldn't have pulled away so suddenly. It's just that I don't deserve your sympathy.'

'You lost your brother, Luc — of course you do.'

'You don't understand — it was my fault. I let him die, and so everything that happened after is my fault too.'

Jenny decided to ignore trying to argue about whether it was his fault or not at that moment. She had seen enough parents in the Emergency Department berating themselves for their children's accidents when they were just that: accidents. Events that could not have been foreseen, that could not have been prevented — not by fallible human beings, anyway.

'What happened after?' To Jenny, this seemed like safer territory. If Luc was keeping all this anger and guilt inside, he needed to find a way to let some of it out, or it would eat him up; that much she knew for sure.

'My parents, they split after Fraser died. It was like watching a car accident in slow motion. Their grief tore them apart. All I could do was watch; there was nothing I could say or do. I could see it in their eyes . . . '

'See what?'

'That they blamed me. They had every right to.'

Jenny remained still. She knew that nothing she could say would change how Luc felt. Words, even well-meaning words could not put a stopper in that kind of pain.

'We'd lived pretty idyllic lives up to that point. It felt like the universe had saved up everything that we had managed to avoid and then threw it at us all at once. It didn't just take Fraser, it destroyed him, and then made us watch as he fought for every breath before he couldn't fight anymore.'

The pain that Jenny had seen too many times before was rolling off Luc in waves. She knew that he was reliving it all — every moment, every decision made — and she couldn't bear to see it. Although the distance between them was merely inches, it felt the size of an ocean. She wanted to reach out and hold him, but was afraid that any movement would rid them of any future they might possess. Very slowly, she moved her hand across the seat again, wondering if he would draw away as violently as he had before. When she could feel the warmth of his hand, she lifted her little finger and linked it over his. He flinched, but stayed still; Jenny wasn't sure if it was because he too was afraid to move or if he was glad of her touch.

The radio crackled.

'Rescue Team leader to occupants of the car, over.'

Jenny lifted the radio so that she

could speak into it.

'Received.'

'We have two teams making their way to you, coming up from the bottom of the ravine. One will come to the left-hand side of the car, and the other the right. Please stay as still as you can until they reach you with further instructions.'

'Understood,' Jenny said, her eyes finding Luc's. She was sure they were both thinking the same thing. Maybe, just maybe, they would both get out of there.

'ETA around twenty minutes, over.'

Twenty minutes. Jenny knew now that she had to say something. If she didn't, she might never get another chance.

'What happened to Fraser?'

At first, Jenny thought she had imagined saying the words, and that no sound had left her lips. She wanted to know so that she could perhaps share some of his pain. The anguish on his face and in his voice was too much, and she knew one thing for certain. It was something she had suspected since that first day, but now she was sure. She had never felt like this before, not even with Kai. She loved him; she loved Luc.

'We'd always been competitive,' Luc said; and his voice startled Jenny, who had resolved herself to the fact that he was not going to speak about it now, and probably never would.

'We were close in age, and all about sport and adventures. Always pushing each other to take bigger risks.'

Jenny nodded, not wanting to speak, afraid it might break the spell.

'We did everything together. Climbing, scuba, mountain biking . . . ' Luc's voice broke on the last word. But he seemed to shake himself a little and pull in a deep breath. Jenny felt certain he had made his decision: he was going to tell her everything.

'We were out biking, just an ordinary Saturday. The weather had been bad, which is normal in Scotland. We were pushing each other, as always, and we came to this trail. I told him no — which was stupid, because he always did the opposite of what I said. I should have known.' Luc shook his head, lost in the memory.

'His front wheel hit something and jammed. He went over, landed head-first. I knew before I got to him that it was bad. He just lay there all crumpled, limbs in odd positions, and looked at me. I knew before he said anything. He couldn't move. Paralysed.'

Luc looked at her, and she wondered if he was checking she was listening. She squeezed his little finger and nodded.

'I called for the ambulance and mountain rescue. They were at least half an hour away. I sat with him, and watched the numbness grow; and I knew what would happen, and I knew that they wouldn't get there in time. I think he knew too, but by then he couldn't speak. But I knew what his eyes were telling me.' Luc shuddered.

'He wanted me to let him go. He

didn't want to live like that, paralysed
. . . But I couldn't. I had to at least try
and save him.'

Jenny closed her eyes at the thought
of making that dreadful decision,
particularly when you had medical
training and knew all the facts.

'He stopped breathing, and you did
CPR.'

20

Luc nodded and turned his head away, banging it hard on the car window.

'Stop, Luc, please,' Jenny said, reaching out for him now, not caring if the car moved or not. She pulled him away, and he fought for a moment, but then his will gave out and she was holding him in her arms.

'You did what you had to, what you've been trained to do, Luc. You shouldn't blame yourself for that.'

'He was paralysed, Jenny, from the neck downwards. He couldn't even breathe for himself. He couldn't talk, but I could see it in his eyes. He blamed me. I should have let him go. I kept him alive — for what? So that he could die of pneumonia nine months later, when for every second of that time he was trapped in his own idea of hell? I should have let him go.'

Jenny could feel the hot tears soak through her shirt, and she knew that she was crying too. Crying for Fraser and for Luc, for all the loss and pain. She held him and kissed his hair, just as he had done for her only days before. She wondered if he had ever cried about it before, because she felt as if the pain were ripping his soul in two. She said nothing, knowing there was nothing to say. That life could be cruel was something that Jenny had seen on a daily basis at work, and in the lives of her friends; but life could also bring the sweetest moments of joy to people, sometimes in the darkest moments. She could feel gratitude that she had met Luc well up inside her. It didn't replace the pain of Kai, but somehow it seemed to balance it out.

For the first time since climbing into the car, Jenny hoped that the rescuers would take their time. Having Luc in her arms was something she felt she could continue to do for all eternity; but, more than that, she wanted to give

Luc the time he needed to feel, something she felt sure he had kept locked away for goodness knew how long.

The sound of voices in the distance made Luc move. When he sat up his face, complete with muddy smears, bore the tracks of tears, but the crying itself had stopped. When he looked at her, she felt like she was lost in his eyes. She reached up a hand to caress his cheek, and this time he didn't pull away.

'I know this may not be a good time. There's not much less manly than sobbing in a girl's arms.'

Jenny shook her head. 'Funny how men think that when the absolute opposite is true.' She thought she saw the ghost of a smile.

'I need to tell you how I feel.'

Now Jenny smiled. 'I thought you already had.'

Luc ran a dirty hand through his hair.

'I know, and I said I would give you

time, but . . . ' He shrugged his shoulders at the car around them, and Jenny had to laugh.

'The universe definitely has it in for us, you mean?'

'Either that, or it wants our relationship on a fast track,' Luc said.

'I know what you mean — '

Jenny's next words were cut off by the arrival of two men in bright orange overalls at the driver's-side window. She had been so focused on Luc that she hadn't clocked their arrival, and jumped in surprise.

'Sorry, miss,' the first man said, grinning. 'You ready to get out of here?'

Jenny nodded, thinking how crazy it was to ask — as if the answer could be anything other than a resounding Yes!

'Of course.' She turned to Luc, and then frowned; there were no men at his window waiting to rescue him. 'Wait, what about Luc?' She turned back to the man, but there was no concern on his face.

'The other team are coming. You just

got the best team who work fastest.'

Jenny was a little placated by his words, but still wasn't about to leave until she knew that Luc was also on the way to safety.

'Jenny, I can see them from here. Go. I'll meet you down the bottom.'

She turned her attention back to Luc, shaking her head; but then saw the look in his eyes, and knew that she couldn't be the cause of more pain.

'Please,' was all that Luc needed to say.

She leaned across, ignoring the exclamations of 'Careful!' from outside, and kissed Luc.

'Meet you at the bottom.'

He smiled.

'We'll probably be there first. Only one of us is a mountaineer. Unless that's something you have yet to disclose.'

Jenny gave him an *As if* look, opened her mouth to speak, decided it could wait until they were both safely on firm ground, and then eased herself out of the now open door.

'Terence and Patrick,' the smiling man introduced himself and his partner. Jenny returned the smile. Now she was out of the car, she could start to feel relief that the events of the day might finally be drawing to a close.

Terence handed her a bottle of water, and she drank it thirstily. Once she had finished, she turned carefully and handed it to Luc, whose hand was outstretched.

'Won't be long, Doctor Luc. You just sit tight.'

'And still,' Luc said, but Jenny was relieved to see there was a grin on his face.

'Probably best,' said Terence, returning the smile.

They quickly helped her to step into a harness, and before she knew it Jenny was attached to ropes with metal clips in between Patrick and Terence.

'This is the easy part, Jenny.' His grin was back, and Jenny couldn't help smiling. 'We face the hill, and then walk down holding onto the ropes.' He produced a pair of thick gloves for her to put on. 'Have you done this before?'

Jenny laughed.

'Well, then, we'll take it nice and slow. No need to rush, unless you have somewhere else to be?'

Jenny's eyes travelled back to the car, where Luc sat waiting to be rescued. Terence followed her eyes and then nodded.

'Rescue One to Rescue Two. What's keeping you, man?' The radio crackled as they waited for a reply.

'A tougher route than yours! ETA five minutes.'

Terence turned to look at Jenny, as if he was waiting for her permission to start the descent. Jenny looked at Luc and they locked eyes. No words were shared, but she could read the message loud and clear: *Go, go* now. She had to fight every muscle in her body to force them to move. She wanted to wait, to be sure that Luc's rescuers were there, but she knew that was foolish. Being rescued was a negotiation. Patrick, Terence, and the others had put their lives at risk to come for them, and the least she could do was follow their entirely reasonable instructions.

'Okay, I'm ready,' Jenny said, taking a glimpse of the steep, debris-strewn hillside. She swallowed. 'At least, I think I am.'

'No worries, Jenny. Patrick will go first; you just follow him, put your feet and hands where he puts his, and I will come after. You are safely attached. Nothing bad can happen.'

Jenny felt a friendly hand on her shoulder, and she remembered herself.

'I know, and thank you.'

Terence shrugged.

'It's what we do, miss.'

Patrick started to move, heading off to the right, away from the car. He was making slow, deliberate movements that Jenny was sure were for her benefit, and she was glad. Whilst it had been days since she had fractured her ribs, the bruising was still coming out, and they protested any sharp, quick movements or when she put too much weight on her right arm.

It was slow going: with such dense foliage, a straight route was impossible. Jenny could feel the sweat running down between her shoulder blades and pooling at the base of her back. She thought longingly of a hot shower back at the shack she had come to see as home really quickly. Patrick stopped, and Jenny looked up from her careful study of the ground.

'Water break,' he said, handing her a bottle. Both Terence and Patrick drank from long plastic tubes that were each attached to a small rucksack on their back.

'How much further?' Jenny asked, her words coming out between short inhalations as she tried to calm her laboured breathing. She tried to see through the trees to the road which she knew was somewhere below, but could see nothing but greens and browns.

'Steady pace? About another twenty minutes or so.'

Jenny smiled. It seemed that even being rescued from the side of a dangerous ravine was no big deal in the Caribbean. Patrick seemed to notice it.

'We'll get there when we get there!'

And they all shared a laugh.

Their merriment was interrupted abruptly when they heard a noise coming from above their heads. At first, Jenny couldn't place it, it sounded so alien. It was high-pitched and grating, and one look at Terence told her everything she needed to know. Something was happening with the Jeep-car combo, and none of it was good. In those few brief seconds she saw the warning looks exchanged.

The radio sparked to life with one word. 'MOVE!'

Jenny had no idea who had shouted the warning message over the radio, but Patrick and Terence leapt into action. Patrick started to half-run through the dense cover, letting the rope run through his semi-clenched hands.

'You heard the man, Jenny. No time for a steady pace now.'

A further screeching sound from somewhere above them told Jenny all she needed to know. Her calf muscles strained, and she knew that if she survived this then every part of her would ache with the effort tomorrow, but it would be a good pain. A pain reminding her that she had survived yet another death-defying situation.

One foot after the other, one foot after the other, trying to mimic Patrick's footsteps. It was hard to concentrate as she imagined Luc on the other side trying to do the same. The only thing that kept her going, kept her mind on the job in hand, was one of the last things he had said to her: *Only one of us is a mountaineer*. Surely Luc would make swifter, safer progress than they had, even with Rescue One's head-start and Rescue Two's harder route.

Knowing that anything but the image of Luc waiting for her at the bottom would likely paralyse her, she kept her thoughts firmly focused on that picture. Luc with his arms wide open and a grin on his face. Running into his arms and being held so tightly that her bruises and ribs protested, but not caring. Knowing the truth about her own feelings and being brave enough in that moment to tell him, tell him everything. However crazy those feelings might be. However much pain she still carried for Kai. She didn't care. She didn't care what everyone at home would say. How out of character it would be for her to be so spontaneous. She knew they would not understand, they would be concerned, but she didn't care. For the first time in her life, she knew truly what she wanted. She wanted Luc, today and always.

Jenny lost her footing, but Terence was quickly behind her, lifting her upright again. She turned to thank him, but his once-laughing face was set and serious, and so she started to move again, vowing to be more careful, not wanting to risk their lives even more than her own.

The sound of grating metal made them all pause and look in the direction that the sound had travelled from.

'It's going,' was all Patrick said before he started to move even faster than before. Jenny was slipping and sliding to keep up, but she could feel that Terence now had one hand firmly around the back of her harness, preventing her from falling too far.

There was a high metal ping, one breath of silence, and then the world around Jenny was filled with noise so loud that her hands found her ears to block it out. A hand roughly pulled one of hers away from the side of her face, and she got the message loud and clear. 'No time!' She scrabbled and scrambled, with no thought now of careful steps. She had one goal in mind: to get to the road.

The sound seemed to crescendo; breaking metal and wood and shattering glass like the sound of a car-crash up close and personal. It reached them . . . and then passed, like a wave on the beach hitting its peak and being drawn back out to sea.

Within a minute, but what felt more like hours to Jenny, the road appeared, and she could feel tears of relief gathering and running down her dirty face. Terence moved to uncouple first himself and then her from the long length of rope. Jenny could see the gathering of vehicles and personnel further along the road, but it was what she couldn't see that made her breath stop. There was no sign of Luc — he wasn't waiting for her, arms outstretched and ready to hear her words.

'Rescue Base to Rescue Two. Come in.'

Jenny could see the face of the rescue captain as he spoke urgently into his radio, and she felt as if the world had tilted on its axis as her tired legs crumpled beneath her and black dots swam before her eyes.

21

Jenny hit the ground hard. Her legs folded underneath her, no longer able to take her weight. Terence was at her side in an instant.

'Jenny?'

Jenny looked in the direction of the voice, but it was as if she had suddenly gone blind. She could see nothing but blackness, and as hard as she tried, she couldn't seem to take a breath.

'Jenny. Look at me.' The words were urgent and Jenny blinked. Some of the darkness receded a little. She felt arms holding her, but knew instinctively they were not the arms she craved. She blinked again, and Terence's face swam into view. His look was pure concern and she felt her heart contract. He knew something, something bad, she was sure of it.

'Luc?' she managed to say, but it

came out as a croak.

Terence shrugged helplessly. She could see fear in his eyes, and knew she was not the only one with someone she cared about missing.

'I'm sorry. Rescue Two ... your friends?' she added, and felt guilty that the other rescuers had been her afterthought when they had all risked so much to try and save perfect strangers.

'I don't know anything. Can you stand?'

Jenny wasn't sure if her legs would take her weight again, but she nodded anyway. Nothing could keep her from finding out whether Luc was ... she couldn't even think the word, so closed her eyes against it and rolled onto her knees. With Terence's arm under hers, she managed to stay upright. She made to take a step in the direction of the rescue captain, the man who could tell her what had happened to Luc. Once again, it felt like the world was tipping forward, and she felt Terence's arm encircle her waist and hold her upright. She took another step and then another, keeping her eyes focused forward, on where she needed to be.

In front of her, everyone seemed to have a job to do, and they were tackling their tasks with the same calm urgency that Jenny saw every day at work. With training, you could force yourself to detach from any feelings you might have and focus on the work in front of you — for a short time, at least. Jenny's eyes sought out the captain but he had disappeared from view. She forced her legs to move faster, and with each step became more determined to marshal her fears. She refused to give in to any feelings until she knew for sure.

'Captain!' Terence had spotted the man in the crowd, and he turned on the spot.

'Glad you are safe.'

Jenny wanted to scream at him that pleasantries didn't matter, but she knew that was unfair. The captain turned his face to her.

'I am sorry . . . ' he began. Jenny felt ice flood her veins, and she stalled to shake her head. This was not happening. It couldn't be. The universe couldn't be so cruel as to take Luc away from her now, not after she had made her decision. But she knew better. Life could be exactly that cruel. She forced her shaking knees to lock and stood up straighter.

'We've lost contact with the other team.'

She watched as Terence and the captain exchanged glances.

'What does that mean?' Jenny asked trying to keep the frustration out of her voice as she knew that the two men were communicating something that she couldn't understand. In the moment she knew how relatives felt when doctors were working on their loved ones and communicated bad news without words.

'We have lost radio communication. Nothing since the car fell.' The captain gestured with his radio to the trail of mud and car debris that was strewn across the road between the command centre and the point at which Jenny and her rescuers had emerged from the forest. Jenny's eyes followed the path across the road and down the much steeper slopes of the ravine. A wispy funnel of smoke told her where the car had finally come to rest.

'Luc was still in the car.' The words caught in her throat, and Jenny felt as if their very sound could suffocate her. A hand on her arm made her drag her attention away from the smouldering crumpled vehicle remains.

'No. The team had retrieved Doctor Luc. They were making their way down an overhang when the car broke free of the tow rope.'

Jenny clenched her hands into fists for fear that she would use them to rail against the captain. Why hadn't the rescue teams secured the car as well as the Jeep? Why hadn't they thought it possible the tow rope, which was surely not designed for such weight, could shear away, sending the car down on its doomed path?

'Any movement of my men near to the car to secure it could have started a landslide.'

Jenny whipped her head round to see his face. There was a look of anguish that spoke of an impossible dilemma, and the heavy weight that decision was now causing. She felt an almost unbearable flash of guilt that her face had given away her thoughts. She reached a hand out for his arm.

'I'm sorry. I didn't mean . . . '

'I understand,' the captain said, and Jenny recognised the expression in his eyes. She had worn it herself before: when, despite their best efforts, her team had been unable to pull off a miracle, when they had been unable to save their patient.

'We are doing all we can to locate their position. It is possible that they have lost their radios.' He nodded his head at Terence, who steered Jenny away to the back of a four-wheel-drive vehicle emblazoned with rescue logos.

'Wait here,' Terence said, before handing her a bottle of water and a protein bar. 'Eat. You will feel better. There are blankets in the back if you get cold.'

He turned to move away, but Jenny stopped him with a touch.

'As soon as I hear anything, I will make sure you are told, Jenny, but I have to get back to work.'

Jenny nodded. She understood. She watched Terence stride away as she sat shivering despite the sun being high in the sky.

She sat and waited, for what felt like an eternity. The activity around her continued, and she felt useless and without purpose. She was used to these kinds of emergency situations, but she had always had a job to do before now. She had never realised how agonising simply waiting was. She tried to keep her mind a blank, but all she could think of was missed opportunities. Times, in the very brief period she had known Luc, when she could have told him how she felt. When she could have been brave enough to put all other concerns aside and be with him.

Those missed opportunities seemed to be taunting her, and she closed her eyes and tried to imagine herself back at home, though even that seemed impossible. Home had always been such a clear image in her head, but now it was a confused jumble, marred by the pain she had experienced. Instead, she found herself thinking of the little shack on the beach, even if it did have parts of its roof missing. She smiled at the memory of Luc climbing the ladder, which reminded her of the fear she had felt when she heard him fall, and then the swift and sweet relief that he was okay.

The shouting caught her attention, and she shrugged herself out of the blanket. She couldn't make out the words — they were an indistinct mixture from her distance — but she could certainly understand their tone, which was one of anxious concern. She searched for signs of Terence or Patrick, someone who might be able to tell her what was happening. She made her way around people; busy with their own tasks, no one tried to stop her. Further on up the road, she could see figures dressed in the bright orange all-in-ones of the rescuers, and without conscious thought she was now running towards them. Between two men she could see an emergency stretcher with someone laid on it. A crowd of personnel approached and blocked Jenny's view so she couldn't tell who it was.

She was afraid now, perhaps more afraid than she had been up to that point. Her eyes were presenting her with cold, hard facts, and she could no longer even try and pretend that things would work out okay. Her feet kept her moving and almost didn't stop when she reached the tight-knit bunch of people. Practically clawing her way through them, she saw that the person lying on the stretcher was also dressed in an orange boiler suit. Jenny took a shuddering breath. It wasn't Luc. It was one of the rescuers, and he was in bad shape. She glimpsed the captain, who was directing the four-by-four to their location over the radio.

'Captain, can I help?'

He shook his head. 'We got this, but we have more wounded coming.' He jerked his head in the direction of the forest, and any relief Jenny had felt was short-lived. 'I need to send two of my men with Charlie. Medevac is standing by, but you can help with the others.'

Jenny spun on the spot and scanned the forest. She could see nothing, the frustration was overwhelming . . . and then she saw him.

He was supporting another man on one side, with Terence on the other. Jenny could see that he was speaking to Terence and his tone was urgent. Behind her, another vehicle rumbled up and Patrick, who had also appeared, yanked open the back door and pulled out the medical kit bag and another plastic stretcher. He tossed it to the ground, and Terence and Luc laid the man down. Jenny took a step forward, but stopped when she saw Luc drop to his knees and start giving orders.

'Open right tib-fib fracture. Have you got an air splint?'

'Relax, Doctor Luc,' Patrick said. 'We got this. Nothing we can't handle. Why don't you sit yourself down? You be needing some attention too.' He grinned at Luc, and then nodded in Jenny's direction.

Luc turned, and saw Jenny for the first time. The look on his face was something that Jenny thought would be burned into her memory forever. Then she was running again before she threw herself into his arms. Luc took a step backwards as she felt his arms around her, and she wondered for a moment if they would fall to the ground in a tangle of limbs, but Luc seemed to regain his balance just before the critical moment. Jenny disentangled herself from him, cursing her foolishness at not checking him for injuries. Luc had other ideas, and held her tight by her elbows so that she could see him but still remained close.

'Are you hurt?' she asked as she did a quick visual survey.

'Cuts and bruises, nothing serious. Going to feel it tomorrow, I think.'

Jenny took a breath for what felt like the first time in hours. The sudden rush of oxygen and relief made her feel dizzy, and she was glad to have Luc's arms on her elbows.

'I was so scared.' She finally managed to pin down a thought and form it into words.

'Me too,' he said, and pulled her back into his arms.

'I thought I'd lost you,' she said into his t-shirt that was stiff with mud. 'I thought I would never get to tell you.'

'Tell me what?' he said, and Jenny felt sure she could feel his embrace stiffen. Her jumbled thoughts fought to process what Luc's reaction was telling her. But it soon became clear as day in her mind: he was pulling away.

'I don't think we should do this here. Not now, when we are worn out and emotions are high.' And with that, he released her and took a step back. Jenny was so shocked that all she could do was stare at him.

'I'll find us a ride. They can drop me back at the temporary clinic before they take you on to yours.' He turned away, but Jenny couldn't let him go — she reached for him, catching his arm. Luc, for his part, froze.

'This is exactly the time.'

Jenny thought she had won him over with that, thought he would turn back to her, but he didn't. He just gently removed her hand from his arm and strode away.

22

Jenny found herself in the back of the truck taking them home. Luc had held open the rear door, and she had slid across to the other side to leave room for him beside her, but he'd closed the door and climbed into the front passenger seat. Jenny could feel embarrassment burn her cheeks at his rejection.

Luc and their driver made polite conversation during the twenty-minute ride back to the site of the temporary clinic. All was calm at their arrival as people worked to remove debris and salvage belongings.

'You can't stay here,' Jenny said, finding her voice at last. 'Come back to the shack, you can stay with me.'

'I need clean clothes and to check in on my patients.'

Jenny glared at the back of his head,

Luc had refused to make any kind of eye contract since he told her they were taking her home.

'Well, I doubt you are going to be able to find any clothes at all in there,' she said, gesturing to the wreck that was Francie's bar and Luc's home. 'Let alone clean ones. And it seems all of your patients have either been evacuated or have gone home.'

Jenny was right: the temporary clinic was empty. She saw Armand rub his hands on his trousers and walk over, leaning down so that he could speak to Luc face-to-face through the open window.

'Doctor Luc, Nurse Jenny! Good to see you in one piece. We haven't found anything of yours yet.' Armand looked regretful. 'Francie and Jocelyn will be staying with me. Not much room for you, but I'm guessing you'll be staying with Nurse Jenny?' Armand glanced at her, and gave her a wave and a smile.

'He can stay with me,' Jenny said to Armand in a mock-cheerful voice. She could see Luc's neck muscles clench, and knew it was not what he wanted, but she didn't care. They had come through too much for him to back away now.

'Just for tonight,' Luc said. 'I have my pager if you need me, and I'll be back down first thing tomorrow.'

Jenny tried to ignore the pain his words caused as their driver got them back on the road. She felt certain that his sudden reluctance had something to do with his brother, and she also knew that if she didn't get him to speak about it today, he probably never would again, and any hope for them would be lost.

The driver drew up outside the shack, and Jenny had to admit a certain level of relief that it was still standing. All she hoped now was that the power was back on and the shower worked.

She hopped down out of the truck, thanked the driver, pushed open the shack door and stepped inside.

'Do you want the first shower?' she called over her shoulder. Her voice seemed to echo around the room, and it was only when she turned she realised that Luc had not followed her. She held back a sigh; she'd been hoping they could talk after they'd both washed, but she wasn't about to risk losing the opportunity to talk to him over something as simple as a shower, however desperate she was to be standing under its cleansing water. She walked back outside and found Luc standing with his hands in his pockets, looking out at the ocean.

'I can't do this, Jenny.'

Jenny moved so that she was standing beside him, but was careful to leave some distance.

'Have a shower? I can go first, if you like?' She hoped that her light-hearted reply might lift the mood, but she was wrong. When he turned to her, all the anguish he had shared in the car seemed to be back.

'I don't understand,' she said, and it came out flat, without any of the emotion that she knew she should be feeling. 'Back in the car, you said you wanted to tell me how you feel. Which is confusing, since I thought you already had.' She frowned now, both at the memory and the fact that she knew she was babbling.

'You're clearly not remembering all I said in the car.' He sounded frustrated and a little angry, and Jenny felt even more confused.

'Trust me, the whole of today is seared into my memory.' She turned and looked out to sea, enjoying the sensation of the breeze on her face.

'I have another day like that seared into mine. I can't forget what I learned on that day, Jenny; I can't. I won't make the same mistake again.'

'And what mistake was that?' She thought she knew where this was going, but she needed him to say it out loud.

'I pushed my brother — we pushed each other — and I lost him. In the worst way possible. And I won't lose you too. I can't.'

Jenny reached for his hand, and was

relieved when he didn't pull away.

'You haven't lost me. I'm standing right here, and if you want me to be, I will stay by your side always.' There, she had said it aloud. She had told him how she felt.

'You don't understand.' He pulled his hand out of hers and ran it through his hair. 'How long have you known me?'

'About a week — and it's been quite a week. Feels like much longer.' Jenny smiled at the thought. She had only known him those several days, but she felt he was the part of her that had always been missing till now.

'And how many times has your life been in danger, in this one short week?'

'A few. None of which are your fault.' Jenny was feeling less confused, but she didn't like where this was going.

'You can't say that. It's what I do. I push the people I care about. Push them to take risks they never would on their own. But you can only take so many risks, Jenny. Someday the universe will pay you back.'

He moved a little way away from her, and Jenny felt like the distance between them had become miles rather than a mere footstep.

'I hate to knock your ego here, but I make my own decisions: always have.'

'Like Kai. Are you telling me that it was you and not Kai who decided to end a marriage that was clearly not right for either of you?'

Jenny fought down the wave of indignation and pain. She recognised this tactic — it was one designed to push someone away.

'Maybe you're right.' The words burned, but she knew that to say anything else would drag them into an argument they would probably never recover from. 'But that changed the moment I decided to get on that plane. Every decision I've made since then has been mine and mine alone. Don't take that from me, Luc.' She was pleading now, and could feel the tears threatening. 'Don't you dare. Coming here by myself was a risk, but if my job has taught me anything, it's that bad stuff happens however careful you are. And if you're afraid of that, it robs you of opportunity and joy.'

'You risked your life for me,' he said, his words almost drowned out by the waves.

'You risked your life for a stranger,' she replied, keeping her voice even. 'And don't say it's different.'

Luc smiled a small smile.

'Don't say it's just your job,' she continued, 'because it's mine too. It's also my life to do with as I will. To love who I want.'

Jenny knew that a battle was raging inside Luc: she could see it on his face, flashes of pain mixed with hope.

'Do you think this is what Fraser would want for you? To pull away from everyone and anyone? Scared that somehow being near you would mean they'd get hurt?' Jenny fell silent. She wondered if she had gone too far, pushed too hard. The old her, the one back home, would never have said those words, thinking it too much of a risk; but now she knew better. You had to fight for what you wanted, fight for those you loved and wanted to be with. She watched as Luc closed his eyes to another wave of pain. She moved to stand in front of him, and slipped each of her hands into his.

'What would you have wanted for him, if you had died and he had lived?' She whispered the words softly, knowing that they would inflict more pain, but also knowing that the question needed to be asked.

'I would want him to find someone like you,' he said, and crumpled into her open arms.

'I'm right here,' she whispered into his hair.

They stood there on the beach, holding each other tight, and Jenny felt Luc slowly relax, slowly let go of a small part of the built-up pain.

'Would you think it unmanly of me if I told you that I'm afraid?' Luc pulled back a little so he could see her face, and she locked eyes with him so that he could take on the full weight of her words.

'Only if you think it unwomanly of me to tell you that I am, too.'

He laughed now, and the sound brought a smile to Jenny's face. She knew that his laughter would always light a fire in her soul. He lifted a hand and brushed a hair from her face before leaning in to kiss her. Eventually, with obvious reluctance, he pulled away slightly, but kept her face close.

'So, what are we going to do?' he whispered.

Jenny thought for a moment.

'We're going to love each other,' she said, kissing him gently. 'And let the universe do its thing.'

Without another word and not taking his eyes from her face, Luc lifted Jenny into his arms. Moments passed, and Jenny felt lost in time. Slowly, Luc pulled away.

'There is one thing . . . ' Luc said, his face suddenly serious, and Jenny felt her heart lurch once more. 'I know it's unconventional, since you are — technically speaking — on your honeymoon, but . . . ' Now there was a glimmer of a smile on his face. 'And I know I said there was no pressure, but — Jenny Hale, I think the universe is trying to tell us that life can be short.' He took a step back from her, and before she could quite take it in, he was down on one knee. 'And so I have a question for you. Will you marry me?'

Jenny swallowed the lump in her throat and knew, without a moment's hesitation, that Luc was the one. And despite the fact that he was right — she was, technically speaking, on her honeymoon, albeit from a previous failed attempt to get married — she knew what she was going to say, what she had to say.

'Yes,' she said, before her tears started to run and she found herself pulled into Luc's arms as he swung her round and around until they were both dizzy.

'Well, now that's settled, I vote we both take the first shower.'

Jenny giggled, not quite believing how much her life had changed in just a few weeks.

'Shower, then bed. I don't know about you, but I'm exhausted,' she said, followed by a mock yawn.

She giggled as he tickled her side.

'Definitely bed . . . but something tells me we won't be getting much sleep, Nurse Jenny.'

'I certainly hope not, Doctor Luc.'

We do hope that you have enjoyed reading this large print book.

Did you know that all of our titles are available for purchase?

We publish a wide range of high quality large print books including:
Romances, Mysteries, Classics
General Fiction
Non Fiction and Westerns

Special interest titles available in large print are:
The Little Oxford Dictionary
Music Book, Song Book
Hymn Book, Service Book

Also available from us courtesy of Oxford University Press:
Young Readers' Dictionary
(large print edition)
Young Readers' Thesaurus
(large print edition)

For further information or a free brochure, please contact us at:
Ulverscroft Large Print Books Ltd.,
The Green, Bradgate Road, Anstey,
Leicester, LE7 7FU, England.
Tel: (00 44) **0116 236 4325**
Fax: (00 44) **0116 234 0205**